I0579077

OPERATION: SLEEPING WITH THE ENEMY

Super Agent Romantic Suspense Series, Book 7

MISTY EVANS

Beach Path Publishing

Operation: Sleeping With the Enemy

Super Agent Romantic Suspense Series, Book 7

Copyright ©2021 by Misty Evans

ISBN: 978-1-948686-42-6

Print ISBN: 978-1-948686-43-3

Cover by Fanderclai Designs

Editing by Elizabeth Neal, Patricia Essex

By payment of required fees, you have been granted the *non*-exclusive, *non*-transferable right to access and read the text of this eBook. No part of this text may be reproduced, transmitted, downloaded, decompiled, reverse engineered, or stored in or introduced into any information storage and retrieval system, in any form or by any means, whether electronic or mechanical, now known or hereinafter invented without the express written permission of copyright owner.

PLEASE NOTE

This is a work of fiction. Names, characters, places, and incidents are either the product of the author's imagination or used fictitiously, and any resemblance to actual persons, living or dead, business establishments, events or locales is entirely coincidental.

The reverse engineering, uploading, and/or distributing of this eBook via the internet or via any other means without the permission of the copyright owner is illegal and punishable by law. Please purchase only authorized electronic editions, and do not participate in or encourage electronic piracy of copyrighted materials. Your support of the author's rights is appreciated.

To Mark...always my love.

"Love your enemies because they bring out the best in you." ~
Nietzsche

❧ 1 ❧

W*ashington D.C.*

ON THIS HOT SUMMER NIGHT, THE FUNERAL WAS IN FULL swing.

Josh Devons swore under his breath, and then took the back stairs to his apartment, avoiding the gathering in the parking lot of bereaved mourners. After ten days here, he was itching to get out of the States. Get back to the life of a spy in a foreign country. He needed the adrenaline rush, the change of scenery.

He needed to get away from the Grim Reaper.

Instead, he was stuck in a political quagmire in the nation's capital, and renting a room from Ace Harmon, his boss's favorite local access agent. Ace's business had experienced an uptick in clients during the heat wave, further aggravating Josh's itch. All this death and dying shit...how did Ace keep his sanity while running a fucking funeral parlor?

Organ music drifted through the open windows as the

wooden steps creaked under Josh's feet. His keys jangled softly on his Red Sox key ring. He rubbed the logo between his thumb and finger. Ball games, hotdogs, pretty girls in Daisy Duke's and bikini tops. When was the last time he'd made it to Boston for a game? He couldn't remember. But that's what summer was all about, and hell if he didn't need that kind of distraction to get over the woman who rode his mind night and day.

If that were even possible—forgetting her for longer than a heartbeat.

Josh reached the top of the stairs and jammed his key in the lock. The outside light was broken; the whole backside of the building, with its dumpsters and peeling paint, looked like a seedy, low-income housing project.

The music drifted away and a male voice began speaking. Someone started crying.

Great. Another evening of listening to women cry. Just what he needed after eight grueling hours with Senator I-Have-A-Bug-Up-My-Ass McIntyre and her Project Disruption oversight committee buddies. Even the argument he'd accidentally stumbled onto in the stairwell that afternoon between the scientist in charge and another guy, hadn't relieved Josh's boredom.

Beats getting shot in the ass, Flynn had said. *And ending up in a Tibetan prison.*

True enough. Both had happened to Josh in the past ten days. The hole in his left buttock where the bullet had lodged, and the various bruises, stitches, and healing wounds he'd received in prison before Flynn pulled some big strings, attested to the fact he'd come close to never setting foot on U.S. soil again.

Which was why the director of spies had yanked him out of the field and put him on the cyber taskforce designing a weapon of mass disruption.

Disruption. He sighed at the irony. His life was the definition of that word.

As he opened the door, the crying down below swelled. An image of his mother doing the same at the kitchen table surfaced in his mind. The echo of gunfire rang in his ears.

Could have been my funeral.

Letting himself into the apartment on the top floor of the renovated Victorian, he closed the door and slumped against it. The Grim Reaper had gotten close this time. Closer than ever.

Fucker didn't scare him. His body was sore, and yeah, he'd had nightmares since the shit went down, but that was the life of an undercover operative. Particularly one who specialized in weapons. Dealing with terrorists and criminals in the market for guns, bombs, and missiles wasn't for pansies.

The room was dark, the security system light glowing softly. The place had no insulation, and sounds filtered up through the registers. Josh reset the alarm, tossed his keys on the kitchen counter, and grabbed a beer from the fridge. Before he took a drink, he rolled the cold bottle across his forehead. At least McIntyre's meeting room had air conditioning. Unfortunately, the man's local economic development plan had not extended to Ace's downtown neighborhood.

But it was Friday night. He should go out, find some trouble to get himself into. Preferably the kind that came with high heels and long hair. And no guns. Definitely no guns.

Hopefully, no poisons either.

He swore as the thought of Naomi flitted across his brain. Damn woman.

Josh strode into the bathroom, stripped bare, and jumped into the shower, taking his beer with him. He needed to clear his head and hanging out in the rundown apartment, listening to the funeral below, would only clog his brain more. After he washed up, he'd ambush Ace from downstairs, call up his Marine buddy, CJ, and the three of them could hit the local bars.

On the other side of the shower curtain, his cell rang. Wiping water from his face, he drew back the curtain and glanced at the screen. ID showed a blocked number. Only a handful of people knew his private cell. His boss and a few friends. The only one who used a blocked ID was CIA Director of Operations Conrad Flynn.

The bathroom was small enough Josh could reach it without stepping out. He toyed with the idea of ignoring Flynn. Decided he was in enough hot water as it was. "So much for a night on the town," he murmured to himself, taking a deep breath, and punching the answer button. "Yo. What's up, boss man?"

The voice that answered was distinctly female. "I am outside your apartment and would like to come in."

Whoa. Not Flynn, unless the former spy was even better at disguise than the legends around the Agency claimed. "How did you get this number?"

"I can leave if you do not wish to see me."

Israeli accent. Breathy voice. Direct assault on his senses. *Might still be my funeral.* "I'm in the shower. Give me a minute."

The line went dead.

And what do you know? That breathy voice and sex-on-a-stick accent made Mr. Happy very happy. Yep, every time Josh heard Naomi Singer's voice, his body responded with a knee-jerk reaction in his lower extremities. Her voice, her body, those big brown eyes...

No need to find trouble tonight. Trouble had found him.

Wrapping a towel around his waist, he stood in front of the mirror over the sink and counted to twenty as his mind raced. What was she doing here? How had she found him? Was this a booty call, or something more dangerous?

Naomi was an expert in both. The Mossad agent had a thing for bad boys. Bad American boys. Josh had made her top ten list. She'd used and abused him before.

And while Mr. Happy couldn't get enough of that shit, Naomi was seriously bad news. He didn't know where her loyalties lay. Didn't know if he could trust her. Scratch that. He *couldn't* trust her. Once a Mossad agent, always a Mossad agent. Behind Naomi's innocent-looking eyes was the heart of a killer.

The Grim Reaper in high heels.

Not the Grim Reaper, he reminded himself. *The Black Reaper*. The infamous female with the Kidon assassination team. She would ruin his career and kill him, if ordered to, without blinking an eye.

Mr. Happy deflated. And rightly so.

"You are so fucked," Josh whispered to his fuzzy reflection in the steamed-up mirror.

And then he went to let the highly-trained, sexy as hell assassin in.

❧ 2 ❧

Sweat trickled down the back of Naomi's neck. Summer nights here reminded her of home. Hot, humid, stifling.

She'd be back in Tel Aviv before this time tomorrow, if all went according to her grandfather's plan.

Project Disruption. The United States' latest weapon could disrupt foreign governments, businesses, and banking structures under a black hat system. A form of cyber-terrorism, Israel feared it would give the Americans too much power, and power was leverage.

Stealing that technology was her mission. Setting up Josh to take the fall sucked, but then, most missions held a component she despised. Her grandfather's blackmail could have been worse—stealing the technology was easy. At least he hadn't ordered her to kill anyone.

That had been her fear—he'd tell her to remove any hinderance in her way, starting with Josh himself.

The spook was lower than a goat. An ex-Marine with big muscles and an even bigger ego, Josh didn't care about the confidences he betrayed or the hearts he broke. She should know. He'd done both to her.

Which gave Mordechai, her grandfather, the leverage needed to gain her cooperation. Not that she wouldn't have done anything for him and their cause, but it was no small relief he hadn't ordered her to take out Josh.

He could have, she knew. As head of Mossad, and their family, he demanded his orders be fulfilled. He wasn't above manipulation, and she wouldn't be on Josh's doorstep except for the fact her grandfather had threatened to expose her darkest secret. A mistake she'd made that had cost her grandfather one of his favorite operatives. Another Kidon member who'd been *mishpocheh*—like family—to him.

The man on the other side of the door had only added to her problems. Mordecai had been more than disappointed to learn of their affair. He'd taken it upon himself to make sure she knew the spy was only toying with her heart, then he'd put her on notice—stop fucking around with Josh Devons or she'd be cleaning toilets at the embassy.

She had one chance to right this ship—and she wasn't going to blow it.

The door to the apartment opened, and there stood the goat himself, a towel wrapped low around his waist. His hair was longer than it had been in Moscow, its wet strands standing straight up as if he'd combed it with his fingers. Drops of water on his shoulders and muscled chest made Naomi lick her lips.

All that naked, wet male. He might have broken her heart and nearly ruined her career, but fool that she was, she still wanted him.

In the scant light, his eyes looked black as they sized up her short skirt, high heels, and abundant cleavage. His gaze came up to her face, lingering on her red glossed lips. "Going to a party, baby girl?"

He liked to call her that. Probably called all his women that. "Are you going to let me in?"

"Depends." His gaze took a slow stroll down her neck, stopping on her cleavage once more. Suspicion laced his voice. "Why are you here?"

Setting hand on hip, she sent her gaze over him in a similar treatment. From the scar on his cheek, down to his chest, lower to the towel. "Why do you think?"

Nothing changed in his expression, or his body language. "Usually, you let yourself in. Tonight, you phone first. Wait for me to open the door. What's up with that?"

"I'm being polite."

He snickered. "Right."

After a long pause, he stepped back, a reluctant invitation. She crossed the threshold, entering the shadowed interior. The only illumination came from the bathroom, highlighting threadbare carpeting the color of camels and worn furniture. "Slumming, I see."

The door closed with a soft click. Josh positioned himself in front of it. "You here to fuck me or shoot me?"

She eyed the equally drab kitchen. "Are those my only choices?"

"The only ones that matter."

His face was now in shadow and his free hand had disappeared behind his back. Holding a gun, perhaps?

"I'm not here to shoot you." She gave him a tight smile. "And I prefer poison, you know. When I kill someone."

"I'm aware. Slow and painful torture is your jam."

It came easy to both of them, this game they played. Naomi tried to appear relaxed. "I heard of your incarceration. How is the..." She pointed at her backside, giving him a nice view of the dress snugged over her hips and ending just beneath her butt cheeks.

"Take that off, and I'll show you my scar."

So hot in here. She wanted to fan herself. Run out and never

8

look back. Instead, she caressed her fingers over the black material, let them linger on her hips.

His eyes took it all in, his arms crossing over his chest. No gun, but playing hard to get like always.

The zipper was on the left side. Grasping it, she did a slow tease down her body, releasing the tightly drawn fabric. "Scars from gunshot wounds turn me on."

His voice came out lower. Rougher. "What a surprise."

The real surprise would be when he realized she'd played him. Just like he'd done to her two years ago. She wished she could turn back the clock. Never fall for him and that scar over his cheekbone.

But she would never live down the embarrassment of telling Mordechai she had failed. Never live down the black mark on her name. She would never forget how Josh had shredded her heart as well as her dignity, and this little side mission—setting up Josh—was her ticket out of Mossad for good. Mordechai had promised, and his word was gold.

Deliberately taking her time, she peeled one strap off her shoulder, gave him a daring look, then lowered the other. She let the material ride low on her breasts to reveal the lace bra underneath.

A bulge formed in the front of his towel.

If only she could still be the cynical, toughened Mossad agent her grandfather had trained her to be. Even though she'd hardened her heart to Josh long ago, every time they met, it turned to mush. The reason she knew she could never be the agent Mordechai needed. She had a soft spot, and those weren't allowed in her line of work.

During the previous encounters with Josh she'd tried to simply enjoy their time together and had hated herself afterwards. Her stupid heart had got caught up in it—the games, the seduction, the lies. This time, she would not revel in baiting him, even if she did want him to suffer for his act of betrayal.

He took two steps and stopped in front of her. Touched her cheek with a finger. "What is it? Hating yourself before you've even done the deed?"

Damn spy always read her so well. Better than any man she'd ever known. Another failure for this elite Mossad agent.

In answer, she leisurely let go of the material, shimmying it down over her hips and baring herself to him.

He whistled softly under his breath. "Garters and stockings. You went all out."

"Speaking of all out." She gripped the edge of the towel and jerked. It fell to the floor, pooling next to her dress. His erection stood at full attention. "I believe you're happy to see me."

He grinned, and the next thing she knew, those big muscles were crushing her against his chest.

3

Poison may have been Naomi's weapon of choice, but she was killing him with nothing more than a push-up bra and a lacy garter belt.

And that little noise she made in her throat when he kissed her? It reminded Josh of all the times they'd been in this exact situation. A rundown room, a hot summer night. Nothing between them but sex. Two years ago, it was Tel Aviv. Then a smattering of secret rendezvous. A growing relationship doomed from the start.

Their affair may have died before it had a chance, but the chemistry between them only grew stronger. The entire entanglement could be summed up by these late-night trysts. For a moment or two in Moscow, Josh had thought they'd left the past behind and started over. Naomi had been caught up in helping him reunite two Cold War spies, and he'd seen an unfamiliar gleam in her eyes. The glimmer of hope that an old romance could be reignited.

It had made her affectionate—a rare thing—and amorous. His own belief they could overcome their differences and forget past mistakes had made him drop his guard. He'd wanted more than anything to believe in her. To trust.

Another anomaly, especially in this business. Trust was incalculable, priceless, a holy grail of undercover operations—always chased, never found.

And then Naomi had received a call. She'd instantly become cold, distant, all business. Didn't take a genius to figure out old Mordechai had been on the other end. Just like that, she was a Kidon assassin again. Trust, love, the building blocks of even a simple relationship, thrown out the proverbial window with the bath water.

Didn't mean he'd stopped desiring her.

With her breasts pressed against his chest, and her hips arching in to his, the last thing he wanted to think about was the leader of Mossad, or what that call had meant.

Now, Naomi trembled under his roaming hands. She ran her fingers through his hair and gave a tug. Her lips parted. Her tongue darted in and out of his mouth, teasing and demanding more.

She never asked for anything. She took what she wanted. His trust, his loyalty...his body. The latter was the only thing he could candidly give.

She stroked his face, his neck, sliding her cool fingertips over his shoulders and down his chest. Why was she shaking so hard? Her body was coiled tight, muscles jumping under the skin. The only time he'd ever seen her so tense was...

After an assassination.

Before and during a job, she was cool, calm, unflappable. He knew because he'd witnessed it, and if Flynn ever found out, Josh would be *excommunicado* before he could say "deep cover." After a hit, she'd be keyed up, the tension finally getting to her. Sex had always been an easy release.

She killed someone before coming here.

Didn't that put a damper on Mr. Happy?

Gripping her upper arms, Josh forced himself to do the unthinkable. His body protested and he cursed himself. He would regret this in the morning. Hell, he already did.

Breaking their kiss, he set her back a step. "What are you doing here, Naomi? Come clean."

She licked her lips, her gaze not meeting his. Her voice was barely more than a whisper. "I'm not allowed to visit my favorite spy? See his latest scar?"

He had options—he could play the game, see what he could coax from her. He could turn the tables on her and find out who she'd targeted and why.

Or he could pretend he didn't know her MO. Take what she was offering and be grateful.

Tomorrow or the next day, when the truth came out, he'd have to live with his guilty conscious.

He didn't like any of the options.

She was so beautiful, so damaged. His rescuer complex couldn't resist.

Sighing, he took her by the chin and tilted her head up, forcing her to look at him. "Tell me the truth, baby girl."

Her intense gaze stared at him from half-lidded eyes. Her red lipstick was smeared. "I need you," she said on a rushed breath. "Just for tonight."

"Why?"

While she appeared to be putty in his hands, he saw the control under her sexy expression. "Do I need a reason?"

"Did you just kill someone?"

Her head jerked, breaking his grip. "What? No."

Relief teased its way into his chest. He wanted to believe her, wanted to trust this...whatever it was...again.

She saw the war in his eyes. "You think the only time I want you is after...that?"

Think? He knew. "Not the *only* time, but definitely up there as habitual."

Her lips curved in a decadent smile. "You're my drug, is what you're saying. I'm addicted to you."

He was no stranger to her trying to turn the conversation, distract him, humor him. "Am I?"

Her face lost its pretense. "What do you think?"

Addiction came in many forms. After watching his dad's fight with alcohol, and surviving his own stint with pain killers, he didn't judge. This dependency, though, might be one for the books. He bet the psychologist at Langley would have a field day with it.

He was a spy, trained by the best, and he called on that now. She wasn't the only one who could redirect a conversation and get what she wanted. "When was the last time you were in America?"

Her breasts, pushed up to great heights by the no doubt carefully selected bra, rose and fell on a huff. She played to his weakness for her with those gorgeous beauties. "Six years ago. My first assignment at the embassy."

"An assassination?"

A dead calm came over her face. "As an attaché."

The classic impersonation for an undercover intelligence agent. "And you haven't been back since?"

"What's with all the questions? Are you my father now?"

Hers was long dead, a tragedy of the family business. "You came with your grandfather?"

She didn't show surprise that he knew he was in town. "He needed me to accompany him. He's getting up in age and feels safer with me as his bodyguard. Plus, he finds my insight valuable when it comes to checking security measures at the embassy."

That much was true, he could tell. Too bad Mordechai was in town for more reasons than that. "He's lucky to have you."

The comment stunned her, but she recovered quickly. "I

wanted to see you, so I offered to accompany him." She lowered her eyes, flicked them back up to meet his, checking to see if he believed her offering. "Happy now?"

He wasn't quite sure.

But it was good enough.

He tugged her close again, kissed her. "I'm glad you're here. I need a fix."

She melted into him, those luscious breasts pressing against his chest, her armor dissolving at their skin-to-skin contact. "Me, too," she murmured, her lips touching his.

The gods save him, he was as damned—and damaged—as she was.

As he laid her on the bed, he only prayed he didn't end up on her hit list—or Flynn's—after this was over.

$$\text{\ae} \quad 4 \quad \text{\ae}$$

*L*angley, CIA Headquarters

Conrad Flynn hated being pinned in.

Signing his name on a document, he stared at the typed version under it, complete with *Director of Operations* beneath it in clear, precise type. What the hell was he doing in this position?

Without knocking, his wife and former partner in the field strolled in, a stack of files in hand. "These are the top three candidates from The Farm." She set them on his desk. "The first would be my pick for you to work one-on-one with."

Conrad shoved the paper aside, eager to get his hands on the files. "Why?" He flipped open the top blue folder and began scanning the man's information. Top of his class at Yale. Four years in the Army, with plenty of special commendations and displayed leadership qualities. He moved to the next page, his focus landing on certain keywords he was looking for.

Julia dropped onto the chair across from his desk. "He's an initiator and quick on his feet. Thinks outside the box—way outside it. His mind is able to calculate multiple scenarios, and he's otherwise..."

Con flipped it closed and shoved it away. "Normal."

"You say that as if it's a bad thing. I thought you wanted this guy to blend in."

Con pushed out of his seat and paced over to the wall. There were no windows in his office, regardless of his status. Langley was a fortress to keep prying ears and eyes out. Knowing him the way she did, Julia had instructed Del to install a large computer screen on the wall that showed various outdoor scenes – the ocean, forest, mountain ranges, and even the desert. Conrad grabbed the remote and flicked through until he found his favorite. "I do, it's just..."

Julia joined him and stared at the familiar image with him. "He's not Smitty."

Maybe later that day he could head to The Farm and hit the track, run off this constant gnawing energy that wouldn't leave him alone. It had gotten under his skin after the Contraband Operation at Christmastime, and he couldn't shake it now no matter what he did. He trailed a hand over Julia's arm, thinking about undressing her under that scene they looked at and doing all the things to her that he loved because *she* loved them.

As if she could read his mind, she took his hand and intertwined her fingers with his, forcing him to look at her. "You still have Ryan. You video chat with him nearly every day."

He stared at her full lips, letting himself remember their first kiss. She was always the antidote to all of his problems. "Europe has him, and yeah, I know we talk all the time. It's not the same."

"Life changes." She glanced at the big screen. "Remember how we would lean out on the balcony as far as we could and catch a glimpse of the tower?"

Paris. It was her favorite spot, and therefore, his. So many memories there of the two of them working undercover operations. So many with Smitty. They'd been three hot-shot agents, protecting their country. "I remember." He touched her cheek, grateful she was back with the CIA, back in Counterterrorism. Their country was definitely safer with her on board.

She drew him to the desk and handed him the top folder again. "Meet with him. Give him a chance. His instructors all say that he's far and away the top in the class."

No one could ever fill Smitty's shoes, and Conrad was no longer in the field, but there was something about bringing a new recruit in to a crucial undercover op that made his stomach tight. He needed someone who was already up to speed, and he would have sent Josh, but the flipping Senator had insisted she needed him. With Zara out on maternity leave, and all of his other best operatives on assignment, he didn't have much choice. He either did it himself— which Julia had put the brakes on—or he found his top candidate being groomed at The Farm, and took a wild chance on him.

His cell phone buzzed and he saw a text from Josh. *Pickup at two?*

Basketball? Why did Josh want to play today? Conrad eyed his digital calendar, seeing that he had meetings all afternoon. He hated them as much as he did being cooped up in his office, and maybe shooting baskets would help.

Julia sashayed to the door, giving him a little extra hip in her swing as she went. "Dinner?"

"I'll be home by seven."

She nodded, blew him a kiss, and closed the door behind her.

He responded to Josh. *Dead Man's Court.*

Josh sent a thumbs-up and Conrad tapped the folder on the desk. Something was up. Something his operative didn't want to discuss at his place, or inside Langley.

He couldn't think what. Disruption was the only item on the kid's plate at the moment, and they'd already discussed it plenty of times here.

He checked the time, made a call to The Farm, and snapped off the screen. The Eiffel Tower at night, lit from head to toe, disappeared.

Life was always changing, like Julia had said, and Conrad couldn't control it. He hated things he couldn't control.

When he walked past Katie, his brilliant assistant, he told her, "I'm going out. I might not be back today."

She rose from her desk in a cloud of flabbergasted annoyance and chased him. "What about the meeting in thirty minutes with Director Stone?"

"I have another one to go to. Tell him it's national security level importance."

With a tablet in hand, Katie tsked under her breath but made a note. Conrad punched the button on the elevator, somewhat relieved he could get out of at least that meeting. He and Stone has a tenuous relationship, more friendly in recent months than previously, but Conrad still didn't like him all that much. "I'm heading to The Farm first to interview Mac McDonald. Then I have the other meeting. If that's done at a decent time, I'll be back around four."

She glanced at him over her readers as he walked into the elevator. "National security, huh?"

He met her stern gaze with his own, channeling all seriousness. "Yes, it is, and no, I can't tell you with who or where."

She narrowed her eyes. "Well, I certainly hope you come back in a better mood."

She turned on her heel and the door shut. Conrad smiled to himself. Katie was one of a kind, and he was lucky to have her, and once he was outside Langley's walls, he speed dialed her favorite florist to order flowers for her.

❧

MAC MCDONALD WAS EVERYTHING JULIA CLAIMED, AND Conrad had the distinct impression he was actually going to like the guy. Within the first five minutes of meeting him, McDonald proved useful. "I see you have experience with sonic and ultrasonic weaponry," Conrad said.

"Handheld portable sonic guns should be available to every law enforcement officer, and CIA agent," McDonald responded.

For the operation Conrad needed him for, that might just be the ticket.

"Would you like to see our stash?"

McDonald's dark eyes lit up. "Damn straight I would."

"Tomorrow. I'll arrange everything."

Leaving the kid, Conrad did just that, setting things up for him to be brought to an undisclosed location the next day, where he would meet with him and further assess his abilities for the operation he'd deemed Mosquito. It could be a simple open and shut case, with few casualties, if any at all.

The sonic weapon would create nausea, vomiting, and even potential disruption of a certain group's vision, their eardrums assaulted by a high-range frequency that would disable them while McDonald stole the necessary information the U.S. government needed.

Shortly after two, he was on a section of blacktop in a rough side of town, two blocks from where Josh was staying. The court had seen better days, and now it was abandoned. The chain link fence sagged in multiple areas, the hoop had no net, and weeds poked out of cracks in the pavement.

Josh was alone, practicing his shots, when Conrad entered. Without a word, the two of them went back and forth, taking turns driving the ball in from various distances, working around the buckled court.

"What's up with the senator?" Conrad finally queried.

Josh was a good operative, but Con knew he felt wasted on this latest assignment. Josh ran a hand through his already spiked hair, then made a three-pointer. Show-off.

"It's not her I'm worried about. We have a visitor in our country we probably don't want."

Conrad retrieved the ball, dribbling for a moment and shifting to set up his shot. "What kind of visitor?"

Josh looked pained, either because Conrad sank it, or because of the information he was about to deliver. "A Kidon assassin."

"The hell?" Conrad stopped moving. There was only one Josh cared about, and it was in all the wrong ways. "What's she doing here?"

"Wish I knew. Could be accompanying her grandfather, like she claims, or more likely he brought her to take someone out. Either way, she's buddying up to me."

"You're not worried you're her target?"

He scoffed, dribbling in place. "I'd be dead if I were."

Enough said. Conrad held back the warning on his lips about sleeping with her. That horse left the gate eons ago. "You have something she wants, and I'm not talking about your sparkling personality. Since you're working on Disruption, could she be targeting one of the committee members?"

"Certainly a possibility."

Mordecai Singer knew about Disruption? Although the U.S. had kept it quiet, the senator and the scientist might have leaked it, or someone on their staff.

That bastard was too clever for his own good. In some ways, Conrad admired the aging Mossad leader; in others, he hated him for making Conrad's job harder.

"You keeping your wits about you?" he finally asked, nailing a basket.

The kid looked away, scanning the rows of rundown buildings to the east as he retrieved the ball. "Would I admit it if I wasn't?"

That was a confession in and of itself. "Fair enough. I know there's a lot of emotional shit between you and her. If you need to talk to someone—"

"A shrink?" Josh laughed up at the sky. "Fuck me. I probably do need therapy."

"I was thinking Julia."

Josh stopped and gave Conrad the side-eye. The ball bounced once, twice, then he held it. "You're shitting."

He wasn't. If he and Jules knew anything, it was how hard your heart could fall for someone it shouldn't. Their relationship had worked out. Most in this business didn't.

Especially when the two involved were more enemies than lovers.

"She's way better at this than I am," he admitted, "but I know a few things about falling for someone who can screw you six ways from Sunday—and I don't mean literally." He dodged, snatched the ball and took a shot, watching it spin around the rim and take its time dropping through the bare metal. "You can have sex with your staunchest enemy. Great, fantastic sex, in fact. You might even believe you can have a future with them—someday. But trust them with your heart? Truly feel safe with them? Never. Even if you overcome all the issues against you, there will always be that nagging doubt in the back of your mind."

The ball hit a crack, bounced away. Josh dug the toe of his sneaker into a divot in the asphalt. He blew out a long, slow breath, as though thinking something over. "Nah, I'm armored up. Nothing to worry about. I won't let her get to me."

Both he and Naomi had been trained to be hyper-independent, to rely on no one but themselves. In love, that vigilance acted as a preemptive strike against heartbreak. "You think your heart is impenetrable, but I've got news for you—no one's is. And if you're girding your loins and fortifying the ramparts, that means you're prepping for battle. Is that what your gut says? That she's the enemy?"

His focus stayed on his shoe. "'Fraid so."

They continued their non-game for another minute, Conrad's brain turning over and over with all the possibilities. It was the scientist; he'd bet good money that was Naomi's target. But why? Why did their so-called ally, Israel, want to take out the person who could help both countries?

McDonald might end up with more on his plate than Mosquito, if Conrad had to pull Josh from this mission. If the assassin was after the scientist, though, it wasn't Josh in her line of sight.

Or was he?

Before he could grill his operative further, Michael Stone arrived with Lawson Vaughn in tow.

"Blowing off our meeting?" Stone shook his head in disappointment. He was tall and broad, a bigger version of the Marine next to Con. "Did you really think I wouldn't be able to find you?"

Vaughn looked like death warmed over, and Conrad ignored Stone to speak to him. "Baby keeping you up?"

The former Navy officer rubbed his eyes. He was lean, and his normally clean-shaven face had plenty of days-old stubble. "She's got a lot of her mother in her. Refuses to do what I say."

All four of them chuckled. Zara was a force of nature, and

Conrad prayed to every god he could name that she enjoyed her maternity leave, but wanted to return to Langley the moment it was over.

As Stone and Vaughn prepared to form a team for an actual game, Conrad pulled his agent aside and lowered his voice. "I'll handle notifying Stone and getting a plan in place for extra security for the committee. You focus on watching your back."

Josh nodded and looked slightly relieved.

His relationship with Naomi was going to be a problem, Conrad knew, and for a moment, he felt sorry for him. Eventually, it was going to come down to Josh or Naomi – one of them would have to get the upper hand, and Conrad hoped it wasn't going to leave Josh dead on his doorstep.

❀ 5 ❀

A ce's Mortuary

THE DEEP BASS OF HIP HOP REVERBERATED FROM THE LOWER level as Naomi climbed the steps to Josh's apartment. The mortician was working on a body and paying no attention to anything outside the building. While he had a camera out front, she knew it didn't work and was only there for show. There was no security at the rear entrance and she didn't worry about him seeing her as she stole up the wooden stairs and let herself inside.

Josh's security alarm was simple to disable. Last night the place had been filled with his presence. This morning when she'd left before he was out of bed, she'd already planned to return and search it. He hadn't left her alone for a minute all night, and she told herself she needed to check his living quarters for any information she could gain on the scientist behind Project Disruption. The senator leading the charge could also pose a problem, so if she happened to find intel or dirt on her, Mordecai would be happy to add it to his collection of blackmail potentials.

The space was as desolate and impersonal as any she had ever seen. This wasn't a home; it was a pit stop. Anyone could be staying here, or no one at all, and she knew that's exactly what Josh wanted – to be invisible, to not leave his mark on anything.

He'd left one on her, unfortunately.

He was one of the best undercover operatives she'd encountered, but she thought his position with the CIA was wasted. With his stealth and lack of connections to anyone or anything, he would've made the perfect assassin. He might be a bit too handsome, she thought, as she eyed the bed where she'd spent the night, the covers still in disarray. The tangled sheets smelled like him, and she sat for a moment gathering them up and holding the fabric to her nose.

The injuries from his last mission had still been healing. She'd traced them with her fingers, her tongue. He looked as beat up on the outside as she felt on the inside.

The only thing on the nightstand was a lamp, nothing inside the drawer or hidden under it or behind it. She ran her hands along the headboard, between the mattresses, and took out her penlight to shine under the bed. The rest was the same—she could find no hiding spots, no electronics aside from the fridge and microwave, and nothing in the trash that suggested he had a secret life.

She checked some of the less obvious locations for him to hide a passport, a gun, money. While there was a stack of hundred dollar bills wrapped in foil and shoved in a plastic bag in the freezer, she could find nothing else. Even that felt like a decoy in case an unwanted robber broke in.

He didn't seem to own a laptop, kept his phone on him at all times, and while she'd attempted to clone it during the evening, the security installed on it kept hers at bay.

The single cheap bookshelf held an assortment of paperbacks, none of which had been read recently from the amount of dust collected on them. Still, she checked the rear of the bookcase, and looked for any disturbance in the dust suggesting a certain book had been removed and returned.

While she worked, she tried to convince herself that this really was about her assignment, and not about simply coming back to this sad, little, one-bedroom apartment because it was her only connection to Josh. She caught herself staring out the window toward the park where he was playing basketball. The buildings across the street were all one story, and she could just make out the corner of the court. She'd followed him that morning, cursing him for not having his own car and using one of the local ride services. She couldn't put a GPS tracker on him, and although she had followed the tiny compact and its driver to the coffee shop where he'd dropped Josh, she couldn't go inside to keep an eye on him. She'd watched the exit for an hour, but he'd never emerged again, probably leaving through a rear employee only exit. She wondered if he knew she'd been following him, or was simply just that suspicious of everyone and normally never came out the way he went in.

He was probably her most formidable challenge, even though he wasn't her ultimate target.

She wondered if he'd brought Emily here, or one of his other girlfriends. It seemed unlikely, considering how cautious he was, but she doubted he needed to. He rarely stayed in the United States for any length of time, and from what she'd discerned, the majority of the women he saw were outside the country.

International romances—the stuff spy movies were made of.

For the longest time, she'd hoped the brief glimpses that came up with his face that involved them were simply undercover operations. It made sense to put couples together to work certain angles, to get into specific parties, circles. But then that call had come, confirming Emily was more than an agent.

Naomi had been unable to prove she worked for the CIA or MI5, but there were so many intelligence agencies, she could have been with any of them. She was beautiful, tall and platinum blonde, big blue eyes and long legs. *The opposite of me.*

Cursing her weakness—one that Mordecai had shoved in her face again and again, Naomi knew it was only a matter of time before she had to leave Mossad, away from the assassin game she'd master as Kidon. She'd lost her edge, all because of a stupid ex-Marine with his arrogant attitude and his flippant jokes.

The problem was, you didn't get out of Mossad. You didn't retire from Kidon. If you did, it was because you were dead.

Her father had learned that the hard way when he'd tried to leave in order to keep her and her mom safe, the thing he feared caught up to him. Mordecai told the story that her dad was killed in a late night hit-and-run car accident, the other driver never caught.

But years later when Naomi devoted herself to her grandfather's cause, she'd come across the information that told her differently. At the time of her father's murder, her grandfather wasn't the leader, but he was high in the ranks and had hoped his son would follow in his footsteps. Having as much power as he did provided a lot of support at his fingertips, but it also created enemies. When her father tried being "normal," it left him vulnerable.

The first person on Naomi's hit list had been the man who'd killed him, a quiet reckoning that she'd never felt guilty about.

As the music thrummed through the floor and into her bones, she pushed away and went through her checklist again. She took down the shower curtain rod and checked the inside – empty. She rifled through his clean clothes, his dirty ones, his shoes – nothing.

Back in the kitchen, she eyed the refrigerator, grunting as she slid it from its position on the sticky linoleum floor and swept the section with her penlight—dust bunnies, dirty coils, and a few items molded to the floor. She didn't want to know what those were.

Damn him. Slamming her hand into the side of the ugly gold appliance, she accidently knocked off the calendar, held up only by magnets. Returning the refrigerator to its original spot, she picked up the flimsy paper calendar and realized it was three years old. She couldn't remember, even with her great eye for detail, what month it had been open to, but as she skimmed through the pages, the yellowed one for September stood out. That had been on top the longest. Whoever had been here at that time had left, and those that followed hadn't cared enough to flip the pages or even hang up a current one.

On the months prior, there were notes, squiggles, circled dates. Even with her high intelligence, they made no sense, and seemed random, just part of someone's life who might not even be alive anymore.

This was definitely a way station for CIA operatives, but it didn't even classify as a safe house.

She could plant a bug or one of the miniature cameras she had tucked inside her pocket, but knowing Josh, he swept the place every night. He'd know immediately that she'd been here. In reality, she only needed this one last hit of him. He was her drug of choice, like she was his.

She'd need to remember the previous night and fortify herself against it ever happening again.

As Ace sang along with the music on his playlist, she took one of the dirty shirts from the hamper and carried it into the living room. She was stupid to be sentimental, and someday it was going to cost her.

As she looked around one last time, she allowed her heart to hurt for a moment, and then she hugged the clothing to her chest, reset the alarm, and walked out.

S omeone had been in his apartment.
One guess who.

Josh stood for a moment, picturing Naomi returning here, seeing what she saw through her eyes as she searched the place.

What was she looking for? He stood for a long moment taking it all in. He imagined her going from the kitchen to the bedroom to the bathroom. The hiding places a trained operative would check, all the nooks and crannies.

Was she looking for dirt on him or information on his current mission?

Sadly, he was pretty sure he knew the answer to that. There was nothing all that incredible about him.

In the doorway of the bedroom, he set down his backpack and checked the camera he'd placed inside a spot just below the knob. He'd disguised it well enough to look like whoever had worked on the pull had created a damaged section under the metal. Del, the nerdiest tech god he'd ever run in to, had provided him with a tiny camera barely bigger than a thumbtack. As Josh synced his phone to it, he watched the replay carefully. As expected, he'd caught The Reaper on camera making her way through each room and coming up empty-handed.

Except for...

What the hell? He rewound the video and watched as she lifted his favorite T-shirt to her nose, smelled it, looked melancholy, and then disappeared from the screen.

She stole my damn shirt.

The alarm on his cell went off, reminding him he was due at DeValdi Industries in twenty minutes. Grumbling, he texted his preferred lift service, grabbed a fresh white shirt and tie, and strode into the bathroom for a quick shower.

Under the weak rain of water, he soaped up good, removing the sweat and dirt from the game, and wondering how he'd managed to get into this situation. He hadn't achieved this level of undercover operation with the fricking CIA, for god sake, by being stupid.

Sure, a few things hadn't gone right lately, but sleeping with the possible enemy was a sure bet he was going down, and soon.

The very thought of Naomi created all kinds of havoc with his body, and he cursed his erection as he turned the stream as cold as he could stand. Goosebumps coated his skin and his teeth began to chatter. She had ruined him, not only his heart, but as an agent. He had to get his head on straight, and his dick out of the picture, or he was going to flush everything he'd worked so hard for right down the drain.

In the kitchen, he grabbed an energy drink and a slice of cold pizza, hesitating for half a second to wonder if she'd poisoned anything. The camera was able to get most of the living area, including the tiny makeshift kitchen, but the angle wasn't right to see what she had done when she searched the fridge. He eyed the food, his stomach growling, and decided he'd take the risk. If she'd wanted to kill him, she could've easily done that last night.

Backpack in hand, he slid the energy drink into the side pocket and munched on the pizza as he let himself out. His ride was at the curb, and as he jogged down the steps, he called Del.

The techie picked up immediately. "Yo, man. I was about to call you. The meeting has been postponed until tomorrow morning."

Josh pulled up and swore under his breath. Between the scientist and the senator, they kept jerking everyone around. "Does Flynn know?"

"The message came down straight from him. He told me to relay a message, and I quote, 'Get your butt to Langley. I want you to meet your replacement.'"

Shit. Josh stared up at the blue summer sky, wondering what the hell that meant. Guess he needed the ride anyway.

"Oh, wait." He heard Del cover the mouthpiece and speak to someone on his end. Then he came back. "Katie says that meeting is canceled, too. Julia just marched Flynn out the front entrance, said they had a date, and she wasn't letting him get out of it."

Phew. Not that he had anything better to do, but postponing meetings wasn't the worst thing. "I need better security on the apartment," he told Del. "I want everything you've got, the highest upgrade possible."

Del choked. "On that place?"

"I'll buy lunch."

The sound of typing fingers in the background echoed in his ear. "You're on."

Josh climbed into the backseat, nodding at the driver and telling him he needed go to an address half a mile away from Langley. He'd have the guy drop him there, and he'd hoof it the rest of the way since he didn't want anyone, not even this stranger, knowing who his employer was.

"Yeah, the works. And charge it to Director Flynn."

"I'm forging Flynn's signature on the form as we speak. Should have the equipment ready when you get here."

❧   7   ❧

W*ashington D.C., Embassy Row*

THE EMBASSY OF ISRAEL TO THE UNITED STATES WAS HER homeland's largest in the world. Their mission statement—at least on paper—was to act as a liaison to strengthen the ties between her country and America.

Naomi relinquished her phone and gun, and allowed herself to be checked for anything else she might use against the diplomats and staff inside. The security guard scanned her for bugs and made her remove a ballpoint pen from the pocket of her jacket.

Nothing like a happy welcome.

And she didn't need any of those items to kill someone.

She walked through the scanner and retrieved her ID before making her way to the east wing where her grandfather waited, posing as a cultural affairs diplomat. Just like her introductory visit, she was acting undercover as his attaché.

She had no idea what his actual reason was for being here,

and really didn't want to know. He and the ambassador had known each other for years, both coming from traditional Orthodox families. Her grandfather still embraced many of those ways, but the ambassador was extremely modern. Although carefully cultivated to give the correct messages, he seemed to enjoy his Twitter and Facebook accounts, and regularly used social media to engage the younger generations.

She'd lied to Josh about being Mordecai's bodyguard and checking the embassy security. In reality, her grandfather didn't actually want her here, and she didn't know if that was because it was a waste of her time, or he feared she'd get off track with her Achilles' Heel. As head of Mossad, it should have been his call where she went and what case she worked, but in this situation, he knew she was the best person for the job.

His receptionist showed her to his private study. A nod was his only greeting. He motioned for her to take a seat, which she did on an opulent Queen Anne chair across from his desk. Powerful people had sat here before her and more would after she was long gone. "Have you made inroads with the scientist, Papa?"

Her grandfather had begun shaving his balding head, and it gleamed under the chandelier. His dark eyes, a match for hers, studied her face as he stroked the gray hairs on his chin. He was a distinguished looking man, aging well, and few knew of his ultimate role in Israeli Intelligence. "That's not your concern. What about the senator?"

She bristled but kept an expressionless demeanor. "I'm keeping an eye on members of her detail."

This wasn't a total lie, and she didn't want him to know Josh was more than a chaperone to the woman.

He leaned back in his chair. "You've never let me down,

except for that one time. This is your chance for redemption. A wise person foresees the consequences."

How many times had he quoted the Talmud to her in one fashion or another?

She wasn't sure if the warning was because he knew she was lying, or if he was simply reminding her not to act out. *Be the obedient soldier, Naomi.*

She missed the days when she was a child and he would play with her. At the time she didn't realize it, but all his games had a strategic angle. He'd read her stories about their history, told her imaginary tales that she realized later were based in fact. He'd been all over the world, seen things she could only imagine, and had built his own empire inside of his homeland's intelligence agency. Nothing meant more to him than honor and family, but his ideas of both sometimes ran contrary to hers.

Something she could never explain to him. "Papa, are you happy?"

The question took him by surprise and that was a rare thing. He sat forward, picking up a letter opener, and tapping it on the desk. "What is happiness?" He paused, but she knew he wasn't asking her to answer. "I don't seek happiness, I seek glory. I seek the safety of my country, my family. Honor to Allah. A man is nothing except for his service to those things."

Naomi hadn't expected anything less, but she still felt disappointment at his response. She'd long believed in that rhetoric, but lately, it felt hollow. She rose to her feet and nodded. "I have work to do, and I'm sure you do as well. I'll leave you now."

Before she could turn, he tossed the letter opener down and leaned back again. "What exactly are you going to do?"

Did he want a detailed itinerary? "I plan to scout the senator's and scientist's homes and offices. If you can't get your hands on the software the scientist has created, and it comes down to me eliminating him, and/or removing the senator from our path, I need to know exactly what playing field I'm dealing with."

She waited for his approval, but it didn't come. His face said he thought her answer weak and borderline insulting. Suggesting he couldn't manipulate the players and get his hands on the software was a dig he didn't appreciate.

She headed for the office door, and he called her name as she grabbed the knob. She looked back.

"Do not mistake happiness for temptation," he cautioned. "Happiness will always be elusive. Family honor and sacrifice is not."

Those bits of wisdom used to stir her, now they fell flat. "I'll check in with you tomorrow. Have a good night."

A smartly dressed man came out of the Cultural Affairs section as she marched down the extravagant hallway. "Hello," he said, falling into step with her, his British accent matching his plaid bow tie. "You must be Naomi."

She blew by him without so much as a glance. She knew who and what he was and she didn't have time for whatever he was selling.

"Very good, then," he called after her, trying to keep up as she punched the elevator button. "Perhaps we can chat later over some good scotch?"

The doors opened and she stepped inside, the first floor button lighting up under her thumb. "I don't chat, and I don't care for scotch."

Once she retrieved her phone and possessions, she made haste to leave, sucking in a deep breath of air once she was outside the gates. She rolled down the window of her rental car and continued to draw on the air rushing past it as she drove aimlessly through the streets of D.C., resisting the urge to go to Josh's.

Not tonight, she told herself. She still had a few shreds of dignity left, and she couldn't justify seeing him as an excuse for researching what she needed to do.

She had one last job, and then she would walk away. How, she wasn't sure. What she would do? That was an unanswered question as well. Would Josh be part of it?

Doubtful.

No more killing, that was what she knew. She swore the vow to herself, chanting it over and over again. Even if it meant her own ultimate death, she was done with this life.

Unsure of the details, but feeling more in control, she punched in the address of Senator McIntyre and called on her Kidon mind to help her get through the night by focusing on the mission.

8

Arlington, Virginia, DeValdi Industries

JOSH WANTED TO POKE HIS EYES OUT, YET ANOTHER meeting that he had to sit through, listening to the senator question Dr. DeValdi about the cyber weapon, and trying to make herself sound more important than she was.

He wanted to run screaming from the building, but figured that might be frowned upon, and he'd promised Flynn he would be his eyes and ears for all of this.

Josh had a strong feeling that he'd been forced into this, not only because of his last screwup, but because Flynn hated meetings as much as he did.

As the senator, in her tailored pantsuit and heels, recited a litany of ethical concerns that the committee had, Josh pretended to take notes. The room was filled with an assortment of NSA and Pentagon officials, along with him and the senator. DeValdi and some of his staff rounded out the group.

Josh was mostly invisible to the assembled members, just another government peon compared to them.

He'd tossed and turned all night, dreams of Naomi interrupting his sleep. More than once, he'd sworn she was beside him and he'd reached for her. What an idiot he was. His bed was empty of all but her scent. She was like a phantom limb he swore was there. Ace, a nocturnal SOB, had heard him stirring and texted him to play Call of Duty. He'd agreed, looking for any distraction to take the edge off his addiction.

An hour later, his butt was numb. Thankfully, the senator called for a break. Josh practically jumped from the chair.

Those that didn't work here had been brought to the secret government installment where DeValdi did his cyber work. It said something when the highest ranking officials didn't trust their own counterparts to know where the genius was located. He ran things with a minimal number of staff who had been vetted intensively, and everyone here knew the dangers of revealing too much too soon to the public. In fact, some of this they would *never* know, if those in charge had their say about it.

They weren't allowed cell phones, but one of the receptionists caught Josh in the hallway. "There's a delivery for you at the front entrance," she said, handing him a note.

Because of Naomi's presence in the country, and her contact with him, Flynn had insisted Josh be provided with a kit that would allow him to check for various poisons, along with a selection of antidotes that could be administered in case somehow, some way, she got around all the security and managed to poison someone.

Over the top? Sure as hell was, but without revealing her identity, Flynn and Stone had made it known to this group that they were being targeted. While most rolled their eyes and blew it off, assured of their own superiority and the extensive security, there were a few who understood that no building was impenetrable, no group of people entirely trustworthy.

Josh was happy to walk outside to the blue van waiting past the fountain and yards of concrete that welcomed folks to what they believed was a non-profit business creating low-cost vaccines. On paper, DeValdi Industries did exactly that, and so the government had taken that and turned it into a bogus entity, giving Healthy Kids International a brick and mortar face.

Inside the vehicle, Josh was surprised to see Del himself. "Don't you have anything better to do, nerd?"

Wiping sweat from his forehead, Del handed him a black box. "Flynn didn't trust this with just anyone, and we're short staffed. Some of those antidotes have to stay at a certain temperature, and there's dry ice inside. Since when do you know how to administer medications?"

Josh shrugged. "One of my many talents. I never completed a residency, but I have some medical training, thanks to the Marines."

"There's a number on there that's a hotline to the CDCs top poison control experts. If you have any doubts or questions, call it and someone will answer twenty-four/seven."

His breath seemed stuck in his chest at the thought. "Hopefully I never have to use it, but I've got this feeling in my gut that things are about to go sideways."

Del looked worried. "I think Flynn has that same feeling. He was like a caged tiger, pacing and yelling this morning. Katie's going to murder him and ask me to help her bury the body, I'm pretty sure of it. And you know what that means... then Julia will have to kill me."

Del adjusted his glasses, his nose shiny from the heat.

Josh punched him on the shoulder, enjoying this moment of camaraderie and joking, so opposite of what waited for him back inside. "It's been nice knowing you. For once, I'm glad to be here and not in your shoes."

"You couldn't fill them, jarhead."

"You're right about that."

Josh took the handle of the metal box and opened the door. The metal was cool to the touch. "Thanks for this. And the new security system."

"Glad to do it. Just don't tell Flynn about the signature forging."

Josh gave him a grin and hopped out. He had befriended a computer geek and a mortician. What was his life coming to?

He was three steps from the front glass doors, the blue van pulling away from the curb, when an explosion rocked the building.

❧   9   ❧

Naomi was sweating in her car when the bomb went off, the blast sending her diving into the footwell. Debris flew across the street where she was stationed, raining down on her car.

When she dared peek over the dash, she was breathing hard, her heart hammering. The four-story building, a modern contraption of glass and metal, had been decimated. She screamed, knowing that the majority of those inside were now dead.

She gripped the door handle and jerked it once, twice, three times, before realizing she'd locked it when she'd sat to surveil Josh and the others. She hadn't been able to follow him, but she had staked out the senator, who was not nearly as paranoid, and sure enough, the woman had led her straight here.

In a crisis, she was normally calm and detached. It came with her training. This unexpected event and the subsequent fear racing through her system made her feel panicky. She took a deep breath, and another. *Don't lose it. Not now.*

Forcing the horrible images her imagination conjured into a dark hole, she stepped out of the vehicle.

The smell of hot metal and burning wood infiltrated the air, clogging her nostrils and making her cough. Flaming materials continued to fall, and ash particles clouded the sky.

"No, no, no." She started to run to the building, stopped, began again. What could she do? The building blazed, smoke poured from all sides, and the debris barricaded the rear entrance that she'd been watching so carefully. The exit a block down from the underground garage remained open, but barely.

The tiniest thread of hope made its way into her brain. Were the senator, the scientist, and especially Josh meeting underground? Was there the slimmest possibility he wasn't fried to a crisp?

Another scream caught in her chest, pushing up her throat and against her lips. This was a planned attack. Who could have done it?

At war with herself, her adrenaline running so high her heart felt like it was going to beat right out of her chest, she climbed over pieces of concrete and made her way toward the rear of the structure. Using the hem of her shirt as a screen for her nose and mouth, she could hear people screaming, yelling, crying. At least a few had made it out. That was a good sign.

Be alive, she demanded of Josh. *No one gets to kill you but me*!

There was no way to get in without dying from smoke inhalation or the collapse of the damaged remains. Instead, her intuition led her around the outside toward the front. As expected, a few people had straggled out and congregated on the wide sidewalk. As more arrived, they clung to each other, spilling into the street.

Groups of others came from across the way and down the

block, racing toward those who were injured, and offering help.

Frantically, she scanned those on the sidewalk, racing between groups gathered there to search for a familiar face. Cursing, her heart falling into her stomach when she didn't find the one she needed to see, she nearly sobbed.

There was a man with a broken, bleeding arm in a suit, a woman whose shirt was torn down the back with something embedded in her shoulder. More with various wounds and some losing so much blood, Naomi knew they wouldn't make it until the ambulance arrived, were carried out by others. She wanted to help all of them, but she wasn't a medic. She had a few basic skills, and understood the human body in ways normal people didn't, but this was beyond the scope of her knowledge.

A crying woman reached for her and fell, nearly taking Naomi with her. Naomi had to help her lie on the hard sidewalk. She wasn't bleeding, but Naomi could see that she was in shock, her breathing coming too short and fast.

"Look at me," she demanded. "You're hyperventilating. Slow your breath or you're going to die."

The woman's huge eyes locked on hers, spacey and afraid, but she stopped crying. As Naomi held her hands, she drew in exaggerated breaths and got the injured woman to mimic her. "That's it, deep breath in, exhale all the way."

She'd never been known for her bedside manner, but her directness seemed to work. The woman's grip was still fierce, but it relaxed the tiniest bit. As the oxygen did its job, her eyes became more focused, although they were filled with pain.

Naomi continued to breathe with her. "Do you know a man named Josh? He was inside with the senator."

The woman shook her head, now able to sit up. "What senator?"

She wasn't part of that group and would be of no help. "Never mind. Keep breathing."

In the distance, Naomi heard a voice that sent chills down her spine. "I need help over here!"

Jumping to her feet, she released the woman's hands. There were so many people in front of her, she couldn't see where it had originated from. There was mostly smoke now, the fires having banked somewhat.

She shoved bystanders and victims out the way and ignored their complaints. Someone turned unexpectedly and ran right into her, knocking her down. She cursed and lunged back to her feet.

Another grabbed her arm and shouted a question. He'd been close enough to the blast, he'd probably lost a good portion of his hearing. She yanked her arm from his grip and was running again before she fully had her balance.

At the sight of Josh, she pulled up short and swallowed hard, all of her adrenaline leaking out of her.

He was alive.

❧ 10 ❧

Josh's ears rang with a high-pitched whine that reminded him of the choirs his mother used to love to listen to. She'd claimed they sounded like angels.

He'd gladly skip heaven if that were the case.

He couldn't get to the scientist, but as he was hauling the senator in her fucking heels out of the debris, he heard something that dulled the ringing and made his chaotic brain snap to attention.

"Josh!"

Sirens came from a distance, as if in a vacuum. Thank god he hadn't been inside, but he'd been close enough for the explosion to rock his world. He blinked at the face he saw in front of him, completely out of place but welcome all the same. "What the hell are you doing here?"

Naomi grabbed his arm, looking him over from head to toe, apparently searching for injuries. "Are you hurt?"

"No. Answer my question."

"Why do you think?"

The senator clung to him, leaning hard against his shoulder, a deep gash on the side of her face leaking blood. Her

48

skirt was smudged with black ash, her eyes vacant. Since they'd taken a break, she'd been in the lower floor bathroom, just off the underground room where the meeting was held. "Where am I?" she asked, sounding drunk.

Josh guided her away from the building. "You're at DeValdi Industries. A bomb just went off. I'm going to get you medical attention, okay?"

"Who are you?"

He feared she had internal injuries from being slung into the porcelain sink, or worse, a concussion.

Naomi grabbed her other arm and they helped her through the rubble, depositing her amongst the other survivors near the street. Josh had seen decapitated bodies, crushed ones, too. It wasn't the first time he'd witnessed such a thing, but it brought back nightmares he thought he'd destroyed long ago.

"What the hell just happened?" Naomi asked above the noise.

He thought that was obvious, but he knew what she really meant. "Someone tried to assassinate all of us."

What was she doing here? How had she found him?

More importantly, was she the one behind this attack?

He didn't want to believe it, knew it didn't fit her MO, but how many trained assassins were running around the city right now? The accusation must have been obvious on his face.

He saw the way her eyes changed from worry about him to disbelief. "I didn't have anything to do with it. I swear to you."

The senator moaned and rubbed her head, the sirens growing closer. Josh checked her pupils. They were tightly dilated and she was starting to lose consciousness, so he tapped her lightly on the cheek and gave her a shake. "Stay with me. The ambulances are on the way." He turned to

Naomi. "Who's in town besides you that could've pulled this off?"

She straightened, indignant. "It's D.C. Trust me, there are plenty of people in this city that could've done this."

He tugged at his left ear, still ringing like an angel was screaming in it. "How did you find me?"

"I didn't follow you." Naomi glanced at the senator.

She'd tailed McIntyre.

There was chaos all around, and he needed to get back inside and see if he could find others who were wounded. An ambulance pulled up, then another. A squad of police cars followed. "This is bad, Naomi. You shouldn't be here."

"I don't know who's responsible," she admitted, "but I'm going to help you find out."

That told him enough. For now, he was going to trust she hadn't been behind it.

He rose from his crouched position and hailed a paramedic. "I've got a woman with internal injuries who's going into shock. She needs medical attention now."

The paramedic rushed over, dropping to her knees next to them. "Can you tell me what happened?"

Josh reeled off the important facts as he knew them. There were others who also needed immediate attention, but he hoped it would give McIntyre a fighting chance.

Once he had the emergency technician up to speed, he started to dash back into the building. Naomi's hand stopped him. "Where do you think you're going?"

"There may be more folks in there who are trapped."

He didn't wait for her response, dragging his arm away from her grip. A moment later, as he fought through piles of debris, trying to move a half-destroyed desk, he realized she was beside him. She helped him flip it over to reveal a woman underneath. "You need to pretend you're dead," Naomi said.

He helped the injured woman to her feet. She cradled her

head with one hand and her side with the other, swaying slightly. He wasn't sure he'd heard her right. He wiggled his ringing ear. "What?"

She led the woman forward around the desk. "Go to ground."

He half-lifted their victim over a mound of twisted iron bars. "Why?"

"Because this is your chance to disappear. If you don't exist, the assassin behind this won't see you coming."

He had a vague idea of what she was suggesting, and on one hand it made sense, but as they led the woman to the exit, he pushed it aside.

In the midst of the commotion, he did what he could to help those in need. Later, when he looked for her, he discovered Naomi had disappeared.

❧ 11 ☙

W*ashington, D.C.*

HER BMW RENTAL WAS IN BAD SHAPE, BUT NAOMI WAS steaming mad, and paid little attention to the dents and burns on it as she drove to the embassy again.

Traffic was a snarl of cars, buses, taxis, and RVs, nearly all in better shape than her means of transport. Several times, it slowed to an unbelievable snail's pace, and once to a complete standstill for over thirty minutes. She screamed in frustration, ignoring the looks of fellow travelers. Most quickly glanced away when she caught them staring, either due to the condition of her Beamer, or the fact she was acting like she might "go postal," as the Americans said about flying into a violent rage.

On the radio, the local news station reported that the senator had died en route to the hospital. Even this far away, she could still hear a cacophony of sirens off and on and knew it would be the topic of everyone's conversation in the coming days. Memories of other bombings, especially 9/11, would resurface to be hashed over again and again on news channels and around workplace cubicles.

Someone would need to be held responsible, and a terrorist group would no doubt step forward to take credit for it. Maybe more than one, piggybacking on the tragedy to gain media attention and entice new radical followers to join their crusade. Regardless of who laid claim to the destruction, Naomi had a sick feeling she knew who and what was involved.

All the permitted parking slots on International Drive were filled. She ignored the orange cones and blockades and stuck the Beemer half on the bricked sidewalk.

As required, she once again gave up her phone and side arm. The receptionist claimed her grandfather was in a meeting. Dismissing the woman's demand that she had to wait, Naomi barged past her and into his chambers.

He was on the phone with someone, probably the Israeli President or one of his minions, his ankles crossed on top of the desk as he lounged in his chair. Upon her entrance, he slowly returned his feet to the floor and sat up. "I need to call you back," he said into the receiver.

Not the President then, he would never be so rude to him. As Mordecai clicked off, he leaned on his elbows and glared at her. "What is it, granddaughter? What has happened to you?"

She stopped at the desk, tapping her finger onto the highly glossed wood. "What's going on?"

He sat back once more and spread his hands. "With what?"

She leaned in, the smell of smoke and ash in her hair. "You know what. Who just set off that bomb and tried to take out all those people working on Disruption?"

Those dark eyes evaluated her disheveled appearance,

inspected her for obvious wounds. "Apparently we are not the only ones concerned with the U.S. having that type of power."

"They're all dead."

His thick eyebrows rose and he looked slightly surprised. "Even your boyfriend?"

Ahh, there it was. There was no point in arguing that she wasn't emotionally entangled with Josh. He knew, and always had.

A new fear gripped her. Was that the reason behind it? To remove Josh from her life permanently?

Cold nausea washed over her. Surely, he hadn't used that bomb to kill all those innocent people solely because she'd had a relationship. "Yes," she choked out. It was no act; the idea she was in anyway responsible for the destruction she'd just witnessed horrified her. "Happy now?"

He clasped his fingers together, face unreadable. "Problem solved, then. In fact, it seems this act of God has resolved several issues."

Rage burned in her veins, revenge, too, but there was no exacting retribution on her grandfather. While he had plenty of enemies, he was still well protected, even from her. "Were you behind it?"

His focus stayed steady on hers. "I sent you to handle gaining intel on Disruption, and to secure the weapon for us. Why would I also instruct a bomber to destroy it?"

A tense silence fell between them as she scrutinized his face. He had no tells, no obvious ticks that exposed his lies, and it was possible he was mixing the truth with falsehoods so she couldn't tell one from the other. "You did send me to take care of it. This was my chance to redeem myself. So where do we stand now?"

He looked down and rocked in his chair. "You failed."

It was like a punch in the gut. While she hadn't completed the mission before the bomb went off, she'd hardy failed. "Extenuating circumstances took the mission out of my hands. Since when does that qualify as success or failure?"

He shuffled a pile of papers and picked up his favorite pen. "I'll find something else for you to do. Back in Israel," he added.

She didn't want anything else, and she sure as hell wasn't leaving until she'd found the answers she sought. She'd given Josh her word. Defying Mordecai, however, was a bad idea. "I was there." She gestured at her dirty clothes, showed him the cuts on her hands from trying to rescue people. "But you knew that, didn't you?"

His gaze flicked up to her, then back to his task. "I assumed as much, since that was part of your job—to keep tabs on those involved. You informed me you were tailing the senator."

"And?"

He gave her a faint smile. "I'm glad you're not injured."

Are you? "I could've been inside."

"But you weren't." His gaze roamed over her briefly. "You appear to be in good health, so go get some rest. I'll contact you with your orders when I've decided on them."

He was so perfunctory, as though he were going to call her with a housecleaning job, or an errand for the market. "Just because the scientist and the others are dead, doesn't mean the formulas and the software behind Disruption won't move forward."

"If any of that survived, I'm sure that's true."

He didn't look at her when he said it, and she suspected that any of the programming Dr. DeValdi had done had been destroyed in the blast. Surely, he had some sort of offsite backup, but maybe that was being taken care of as she lingered. She turned on her heel and marched for the door. She was going to check.

"We should have dinner together tonight," her grandfather called.

That was the last thing she wanted to do, but she knew how to fake just about anything. "Sounds lovely. See you then."

Out in the hall, she kept her expression stoic, refusing to let anyone see the traitor she was about to become. She left the building, got in her car, and didn't let herself break down until she was miles away.

❧ 12 ☙

A*ce's Mortuary*

THE SKINNY KID WAS A RUNNER FOR ACE, AND WHEN HE appeared on Josh's doorstep, the whites of his eyes were showing, along with a sheen of sweat that suggested someone had scared the bejesus out of him.

"What's up?" he asked the boy.

One terribly thin arm held out a piece of paper. "She said to give this to you and tell you that you can't stay here no more."

Josh handed him the freshly made sandwich in his hand—he hadn't even taken a bite of it yet—and accepted the note. "Who?"

But the kid, absconding with the food faster than lightning, was already dashing down the stairs and racing off to his hangout, blocks away.

Unfolding the paper, he noticed the embassy's letterhead

and read the perfunctory script. *Meet me at cemetery. Sundown. Come alone. Wear disguise.*

The nearest graveyard was a Catholic one two miles north. Josh debated with himself, but he was a hot mess anyway. His head was killing him, his back, too. He had burns on his fingers and arms from rescuing people, and Flynn had made him see a doctor who treated certain operatives and kept his mouth shut about them and their wounds. That was a big neon sign that his boss was thinking along the same lines as Naomi.

She'd told him to pretend to be dead, and Flynn had released his name among those killed in the bombing. A few of the identities had been kept out of the public eye, but his had been front and center, along with the scientist, who really was deceased, and the senator as well.

It was like putting the layers back on an onion—covering up this, blanketing that, suppressing details here and there. A statement had been released claiming that it was a gas explosion and not a deliberate act of terrorism. It might fool the general population, but Josh was positive those who ran in certain circles knew exactly what had happened.

Crumpling the note, he launched it like a basketball at the garbage can and considered what he could do for a disguise as it sank. He had jeans and T-shirts, his dress clothes, a ball cap. Not exactly rocking the camouflage, but he hadn't been working undercover, so there was no need. With his training, he could use about anything to conceal his looks if necessary, but it would take more time and energy than he could muster.

Going all the way to Langley wasn't appealing either. While the stores of disguises there would make it easy pickings, getting there and back in time to meet her at sundown would be difficult.

An idea hit when he heard Ace swearing at the game he was playing. Josh bombed into the mortician's place, startling him and stealing a canister of cheese balls from his kitchen counter.

As Josh munched on the junk food, he listened to Ace complain as he rifled through the man's closet. "My man, you can't pull off my look. It's one of a kind, just like me. And you're getting cheese dust on everything!"

Ace was at least forty pounds lighter and a few inches shorter, but Josh found an assortment of items he would never be caught dead in, including a light blue velvet tracksuit. White stripes decorated the sides of the arms and legs that would match the white tennis shoes he found in a pile at the back. They were tight on his feet, but close enough.

He also noticed several women's garments. "Where's your girlfriend?" he asked. "Carrie, isn't it?"

Ace's gaze darted to the side. "Visiting her aunt. And it's pronounced Car-*ee*, Cari, not *Care*-ee."

"You two have a fight?"

"What?" He grimaced. "Nah. She just...needed space."

A couple of gold chains and a black velvet hat completed the look. He didn't want to call attention to himself, and yet, in this neighborhood, he would blend in. "Women. Who can understand them?"

"Right?" Now the guy met his eyes, nodding. "Big Mike got married and she was all 'did you see that ring?,' 'how romantic,' she's a lucky woman.' So I'm thinking, Ace, you got to up your game. Them is hints."

Michael Stone, the Deputy Director, had proposed at Christmas to his girlfriend, the highly sought-after expert on terrorists, Dr. Brigit Kent. He'd also married her on the spot in his home when she'd said yes. Josh hadn't been at the party, but he'd sure heard about it in the halls of Langley.

A guy like Stone was suave and Josh suspected he knew all the right moves. Josh and Ace were at the other end of that spectrum. Like two dogs who didn't know how to swim, they were barely keeping their noses above water.

The heaviest of sighs left Ace's full lips. "I don't got no money, man. I mean, look around. The death business is a constant one, but inflation and all. Nobody in these parts has cash to spend on *dyyyying*." He exaggerated the word.

If he hadn't been in a time crunch, he would have sat down and finished the snack. He hardly thought Ace could help him with his own romantic entanglement, and yet, commiserating with a fellow schmuck held appeal. "So you *didn't* propose?"

"I sure as hell did. Romantic dinner and all. The ring was small but nice. Got it over at the pawn shop. Had filigree or some frivolous stuff on the band. Thought she'd dig it, you know? She likes all that vintage crap."

He wiped his fingers on a kitchen towel and leaned on the counter. "I take it she didn't."

"Nah." Ace waved it off. "Said I was crowding her. Next thing I know, she's bailing on me, saying she's got to visit her auntie."

The stiff silence told Josh neither of them knew exactly what that meant, but he felt for the guy. It was obvious from his face, he was devastated. "I think she's embarrassed to marry someone like me."

"A mortician?"

Ace gave him a chastising look. "Not exactly what you put on your dating app bio, you feel me? I ain't got no girls flocking to me like you do."

If Stone or Flynn were here, they'd have some smooth thing to say to make Ace feel better. Josh had no clue what that might be. "I don't have women chasing after me."

"Man, I heard you go at it the other night with that bad girl. Had to put my noise-cancelling headphones on you two were so loud."

Josh winced. "Sorry. But that was once. One woman."

"I bet you've got plenty of them, Mr. Spy Man."

"Actually, it's just her. She *is* a bad girl, especially for me to be involved with, but I can't get her out of my head. Since the first time I saw her, I've been screwed."

"She's screwing you, all right." He grinned at his joke. "She the one?"

Yes. "Maybe."

"I gotta ring if you need it."

Josh laughed. He straightened and motioned at himself. "Well, what do you think?"

Ace stood back, arms crossed, and gave him a reluctant nod. "Okay, I see the vibe you're going for. Still think it ain't gonna work."

"I'll be lucky if I'm not killed by the time I get to the cemetery."

"A white dude in that getup is fair target," Ace agreed. "You better let me drive you."

Ace's wheels consisted of a 1970s Caddy with a lift kit. Talk about standing out.

"We take the hearse," Josh said, hefting his backpack on his shoulder.

"What?" His scrunched up face said it all. "Why?"

"It won't look out of place, idiot."

Ace shook his head and beeped the key fob, unlocking the black vehicle. "And you won't?"

Josh climbed into the passenger seat, the once tan interior worn and stained. "Keep your mouth shut about this, okay?"

Ace chuckled. "Are you kidding me? I already took your picture. Filed it in top-shelf blackmail material, my man."

Josh cuffed him on the side of the head. "Try it, Ace, and you'll end up six feet under."

Ace cowed and rubbed his ear. "Jesus, you're as bad as Flynn."

Dusk was falling, shadows thick thanks to a cloudy sky. She hadn't give him any instructions on where in the cemetery to look for her, and the place was a big one, winding over several acres of ground.

Just like her to make him work for it.

Places such as this didn't bother him as it did most folks. He didn't believe in ghosts and death held no fear for him. He'd been to plenty of Catholic funerals and burials, his mother's faith a deep source of comfort to her. Even now, when he saw a particular saint or angel statue, it would remind him of the reverence he had for such things because of her, not any belief of his own.

Since the aftermath of the explosion, he'd tried to keep his mind off Naomi, off what she'd said and how she'd helped him at the site. He knew she wasn't behind it, but his training made him so paranoid, believing in anyone, much like believing in religion, was like asking him to jump out of an airplane with no parachute. He needed proof.

He hated flying, and he especially hated jumping out of planes.

Vehicles weren't allowed inside the gates, and Josh told Ace to get lost.

"You stupid, bro? Don't be walking back to the funeral parlor in that getup after dark."

Josh sighed. "I'll get a ride, and if anyone comes asking about me –"

"I don't know who you are, I've never seen you in my life, yada yada yada. I know the drill."

Josh exited the hearse and watched as Ace pulled away before he turned to scan the tombstones. If she did want to kill him, this would be a good place to do it, but he knew she wouldn't have called him here for that.

He eventually found her behind a large crypt that belonged to a family named Mahoney. She looked at his getup, but refrained from making fun of him, and he was both disappointed and glad. She was shook up, he could tell, and he had to force himself not to reach for her.

"I've already stated for the record that I had nothing to do with the explosion, but I'm restating it. I had no indication that something like that was going to happen, and I want to make sure you believe me."

He leaned against the concrete and nodded. "I believe you."

Her face flashed with relief, then doubt. "You do?"

The tracksuit was hot, and he wanted to peel it off, and throw on the cotton shirt he had in his pack. He wiped a trickle of sweat from the back of his neck. "Why am I here, Naomi?"

"Was there an off-site backup of DeValdi's work?"

She was still after it then. For her grandfather? For the ambassador? For Israel's president? "I don't have clearance on that subject. My sole involvement was to watch the senator's back. Lotta good that did her."

Her gloved hands fisted. "It wasn't your fault."

"Wasn't it?"

A slight shake of her head. "I saw they listed you as one of the dead."

"My boss thought it advantageous going forward."

She seemed pleased, her fists relaxing. "I'm investigating, and I won't get in your way because I know you are, too, but this is the last time you'll see me in person."

His guts clenched and he took a step toward her, fearing she was about to run off. "Tell me what you know."

She shook her head. "I don't have hard proof, yet. Only suspicions and that's not enough."

She had no obvious outward ties to what had happened, and while he'd heard some people claim she was an angel in the aftermath when she helped them, he knew no one could

ID her. She was a ghost in the wind, like always, and now he was as well. He hated to suggest it, but in reality, it made sense. "Working together would be more efficient."

Her surprise was obvious, and then she chuckled. "It could get me killed."

That was true, and he felt guilty because he hadn't considered that. Her grandfather was no one to mess with, and like Flynn, he seemed to know every move people made before they even made it. "I understand."

"I'll have to find ways to feed you any information I discover, so be alert, and keep your head down. Don't assume you're home free because the world thinks you're dead."

It almost sounded as if she really cared about him, and Josh reached out and gave her a playful punch against the arm. "I happen to have training in covert operations, in case you hadn't figured that out."

His attempt to lighten the mood fell flat, and maybe it was the shadows playing games with his eyes, but he thought he saw her lips tremble a moment before she once more stiffened her spine and turned away. "Goodbye, Josh."

He almost called after her, but he didn't know what to say. Don't go? Thanks for helping me? What do I do now?

He watched her until he couldn't see her anymore, the encroaching night swallowing her up.

❧ 13 ❧

S t. *Anne's Cemetery*

"Ace called. He wants his clothes back." Flynn put the car in drive.

Josh had tried texting a new ride service, prepared to set up a bogus identity, but had found his phone disabled. His boss was waiting for him at the gates. The sedan was tan, boring, and not Flynn's style, nor was he alone. Julia and another man greeted Josh as he got in.

He slouched in the backseat, the cheap upholstery the same shade as the paint job. "I was desperate."

"It's a great disguise," the man said, holding out a hand. "Our previous meet and greet got canceled. I'm Mac McDonald."

He tossed the ridiculous hat onto the seat between them. "Josh Devons. Heard you're my replacement."

McDonald had the grace to look sheepish as they shook. "I'm eager to get in the field."

Julia handed Josh a manila envelope over her shoulder, then adjusted the radio controls. "Your new ID. Also the official obituary. I notified your cousin in Colorado and your aunt in California of your passing, and told them it happened while you were on State Department business."

They probably didn't remember he existed. He rifled through the envelope, not bothering to read his obit, and withdrew a new driver's license with a backstop identity—Justin Delvin. Easy to remember. "We're not close."

Del came over the radio, and Josh realized this boring vehicle that looked like thousands of others in the tri-state area was kitted out with some of the Agency's best gadgets. "You're previous phone and laptop have been disabled. New ones are linked to the Delvin name, and although the legend is thin at the moment, I'm working on it. Hopefully this is all cleared up before anyone starts digging into Delvin or his history."

Josh tucked the license and new phone into his backpack. "Thanks. I assume you want the scoop on what Naomi said."

McDonald handed him a steel gray bag with dozens of pockets. "Better trade that old one out. Can't take any chances, you know."

Josh was both annoyed at the fact he should have thought of that and respected the fact Flynn had found someone nearly as paranoid as he was. Maybe McD *was* a good replacement for him.

Accepting it, he noticed in the rearview that Flynn looked pleased. "Does she know who did it?"

Shaking his scant belongings out of the old carrier he'd grown fond of, he kept his head down as he transferred them to the new bag. It was pretty nice, yet totally understated like the car. Put him in a crowd and it wouldn't call attention to itself, even though it was worth way more than the average backpack. Along with a phone charger, GPS locator, Swiss

Army knife, money, and credit cards, it also held a first aid kit, gun, and ammunition. A passport showed the same Delvin ID, and there was cash in foreign denominations tucked next to the US bills. Best of all? There was a change of clothes—*his* shirt and jeans. Josh had to admit McD was thorough as well as smart.

"No." He peeled off the tracksuit top and tugged on his own, beautiful T-shirt—the Def Leppard tour one that had been washed so many times the graphic had faded to a ghostly version. It was his favorite. "But she has suspicions and claims she'll give me any evidence she uncovers."

"Do you believe her?" Julia queried.

Did he? "Yes. She's between a rock and hard place right now. I can't figure out exactly why, but she was there at DeValdi Industries for a reason, and I don't think it was solely because of me. Her grandfather wants Disruption, we know that, but why send her to get it? She's an assassin, not a computer geek."

"She has cyber training," Del aid.

McDonald piped up. "Her hacking skills aren't on par with say, Del's, but she could still be a potential problem if given the right access to that software."

"But we knew she was in the country," Julia said. "It's like she purposely showed up on your doorstep, Josh. We could easily put two and two together and follow the theft to Mordecai and Israel. That's sloppy intelligence, and if we know anything about them, they're not sloppy."

Flynn seemed to drive aimlessly, but Josh knew he never did anything without a goal. "We're missing a piece of the puzzle. We have to think outside of this box Naomi has constructed."

"She's a distraction," Josh said, knowing he'd been had. "To keep me off the scent of the bomber, but even she didn't know about that. She was being used."

Flynn nodded. "Possible. Or she was purposely setting you up to take the fall for something. Like her, you have a decent amount of cyber skills yourself."

A tense silence fell and Josh knew Flynn was dropping breadcrumbs to see which of them—him or McD—got to the finish line first.

Unfortunately, he knew that was only the start of this race. "If she stole the Disruption plans, Israel would need to put the blame on someone else." He jammed his old backpack under the seat and swore softly. "Who better than someone on the inside watching the senator's back?"

Julia sucked in a soft breath as Flynn smiled again. "You gotta hand it to Mordecai, he's crafty. He knows about your relationship and found a way to use it against her."

"But what about the bomber?" McDonald asked. "Why destroy the plans for the weapon if they only wanted to steal it?"

"We have another player in the ring," Flynn said, taking an offramp that led to a car rental place. "Either Mordecai is teaching Naomi a lesson, or he plans to take her out of the equation entirely."

"We have to do something," Julia said.

Josh was about to say the same thing.

Flynn parked the sedan and turned to Josh. "Rent a car and find your girl. She's most likely in danger."

"That might be a problem," Del added.

"Why?" Flynn, Josh, and McDonald all asked in unison.

"From the device you put on her car, Director, it shows she's in a very dangerous and extremely secure location."

"You put a tracker on her?" Josh's hand went to the door handle, and he demanded of Del. "Where is she?"

Del sighed, and Josh imagined him pushing his glasses up his nose. "Like I said, an extremely secure location. She's at the embassy."

❧

Embassy of Israel to the United States

Naomi controlled her breathing as she broke into her grandfather's office. Keeping her heartrate even was imperative in any criminal undertaking, as was acting as though she were doing something completely normal.

He was out—that was all his receptionist would tell her. Naomi had pretended to leave again, waiting until the woman took a break to pick the lock.

Fifteen minutes, that's the max she had. She set her watch for five.

The room was silent, cool from the air conditioner, and smelled like Mordecai's favorite figs and cigars. Funny how those aromas were so familiar, she never noticed them when he was present. In his absence, however, they hung in the air like ghosts, standing in for him.

She skimmed the top of the desk, neat files on top of his calendar. None were marked top-secret, or with the name of Project Disruption. She didn't expect it to be that easy, but it would've been nice.

The antique leather of his chair gave a muffled squeak as she sank into it and attempted to gain access to his computer files. It was a comfortable seat, high-quality, but broken in.

The firewall was a challenge and took several precious minutes to defeat. She hurriedly scanned through the recent files he'd opened. Nothing jumped out at her and she slammed her hand down on the desk, frustrated. There was no mention of Disruption, DeValdi, or the senator in anything she could see. She closed her eyes a moment, trying to think like him. Even if he felt safe enough to use the obvious terms, he wouldn't. He was far too careful for that.

Resuming her hunt with the two minutes left, her gaze fell to the calendar on his desk. He was old-fashioned enough to like paper copies, and a notation in yesterday's square made her pause. Rahab—a name she had shoved into a mental hole, hoping to never think about again. Why had he written *that* in his calendar?

She combed her memory. Was it the anniversary of her death? No, that she was sure of. Her grandfather had treated the Mossad agent almost as though she, too, were his beloved granddaughter.

My one mistake.

Sentimentality didn't fit Mordecai, however, and Naomi filed it away for now. She had to leave before the receptionist returned, and she didn't have time to copy any files. Doubtful Mordecai would leave damning information on it anyway, no matter how much she'd hoped for the uncomplicated means to retrieving solid evidence.

But he was getting old, and his memory wasn't as good as it used to be. If he was involved in the terrorist act, even remotely, there had to be a trail between him and the bomber.

Exiting, she slid into a nearby dark alcove as the receptionist returned from her break, humming with the piped in music overhead. Once she had headphones on and was typing away at her computer, Naomi slipped off down the hall.

Colin Barber caught up to her just outside. "We meet again."

Like last time, she kept walking.

He hurried to keep up. "You've been around a lot the past few days."

Performing a repeat of the elevator exchange, she pushed the round button and tapped her foot, waiting for it to open. "Is there something I can do for you?"

It was a rhetorical question she didn't expect him to

answer, hoping the tone of her voice suggested that he should fuck off.

He didn't take the hint and followed her on to the elevator. "We haven't been properly introduced. I'm Colin."

He held out a hand and she looked at it with disdain. "I'm not interested."

He looked slightly abashed. "I admire your grandfather and I was just trying to—"

The doors closed. "I'm aware of what you're trying to do. I also know you have a reputation, and your last name isn't Barber. Why don't you go back to the British Embassy and leave the rest of us alone?"

The unexpected brush off and revelation that she knew who he really was under that carefully cultivated ID MI5 had given him years ago, made for an uncomfortable situation in the enclosed space. She kept her hard gaze locked on his, seeing if he would look away, or keep up the ridiculous act.

He held her eyes. Then realizing the game was up, he leaned against the wall and smiled once more. This one was shrewd, calculating. "Perhaps we could talk shop over dinner?"

Thankfully the elevator was swift and brought them to the first floor before she had to kill him. "I don't talk shop with anyone, and I have no desire to go to dinner with you. Please don't ever speak to me again."

She exited and walked to the desk. As the guard handed over her belongings, she saw she'd missed a text from Josh. It was actually an unknown number, but she knew from the emoticon he'd used of a skull and cross bones, that he was letting her know how to contact him.

Smiling to herself, she pocketed it and was about to walk out when two other men in dark jackets stepped forward. Both wore guns. One tapped an earpiece and spoke into it. "Got her."

Each of them grabbed an arm. "Come with us," the man who'd tapped his earpiece said.

She tried to break free but their grips were solid. The other guard dug a thumb into her wrist. "What's this about?"

"You're needed downstairs."

That area was for interrogations. She fought against the man's grip. "Let me go. You've confused me with someone else."

Between them, they practically lifted her off her feet and carried her across the beautiful tiled floor into a hidden door on the right. She was unceremoniously escorted down two flights of steps, kicking and yelling. "I'm Mordecai Singer's granddaughter! I want to speak to him. Now!"

They ignored her demands, forcing her into a hallway with multiple metal doors and no windows. The doors hid bare rooms; one was marked 'For Authorized Personnel Only.'

Had they realized she'd hacked into her grandfather's computer? Was Barber pulling some kind of prank on her because of her rudeness?

Either way, this part was bad news. Most of the world didn't realize it existed, but there were those who went into these rooms and never came out, except in a body bag, quietly disposed of in some random forest or river.

The one who'd dug his thumb into her wrist unlocked the door to a room, and her fight instincts kicked in full force. She used an elbow and then a knee to take his cohort to the floor, stripping him of his gun and knocking him unconscious. Pointing it at the first, she watched him raise his hands in surrender, but she could see he was ready to tackle her if given the chance.

He outweighed her by enough to make a wrestling match challenging. Shooting him would be the easiest way to take care of him.

Firing would bring everyone running and shut down the entire place in three seconds. She'd never escape. So when she egged him to attack and he responded, she used the gun to do significant damage to his nose cartilage and jaw, then kicked him in the balls.

He fell, dazed and in pain, sneering at her. He attempted to stagger to his feet but she was on him in a second, stealing his gun and using both weapons to knock him out.

The second man regained his composure, reaching for her leg. A kick to his solar plexus left him gasping for air and she finished him off with a blow to his head.

It really hadn't been much of a challenge, and with her adrenaline running high, she was almost disappointed. She really needed to talk to her grandfather about the security here – it was lackluster at best.

If she ever spoke to him again.

Scrambling back up the stairs, she dialed the unknown number, listening to it ring. There was only one way out of the stairwell, and that would send her back across the entry space, and the security guard. It was either that, or run through the labyrinth here to try and find the rear exit.

"We need to meet," came Josh's voice as soon as he answered.

"I'm in trouble," she blurted. "I'm at the embassy and they're trying to detain me. I don't know why." She stood in the doorway looking at the expanse between her and the glass doors of the entry.

"Do you need me to come in and get you?"

What a ridiculous idea. He was across the city, and he couldn't waltz into the Israeli Embassy and demand they turn her loose. "I don't have time to wait for you. I have to get out of here now, but I'm not sure where I'm going from here."

His next words brought a smile to her lips. "If you can get out of the building, you're home free. I'm already outside."

❧ 14 ❧

She wasn't going to make it.

Naomi hit the side door that opened into a small courtyard, setting off alarms. She ran for the gates, scanning the street for him.

It was everything Josh could do to sit in the car instead of jumping out and trying to help.

McDonald was next to him, punching buttons on the contraption in his hands. "This should help. She'll have to go up and over the gate but I've disabled the current."

"It's electrified?" Josh could see where this guy might come in handy. "And the security cameras?"

Flynn would kill them if they were caught on camera. "All they're seeing is fuzz," McD assured him. We're safe."

Naomi was only a few feet from the iron fencing, but a security guard was on her heels. Upstairs, he saw a man in a window watching. Embassy windows were always covered, but the shade was open and it wasn't Mordecai, but someone with a keen interest in what was happening.

Josh gripped the steering wheel, knuckles white. "Why aren't they shooting at her?"

He already knew the answer but McDonald confirmed it. "The head of Mossad doesn't want his granddaughter shot out in the open, nor does the ambassador want that kind of publicity. Their orders are to subdue, not kill."

The guard caught her by the back of her shirt and Josh's teeth clamped together. She turned and fought, striking the man in the face and his head in rapid succession so many times Josh couldn't follow her movements.

Then she was up and over the fencing, as if knowing that was her only chance. She came down hard on their side and yelped.

He had to do something, his hand going to the door. "Come on, come on."

McDonald stopped him. "She's okay. Look."

It was a hard fall, but she scrambled to her feet. She limped as she closed the distance to the car, determination etched on her face.

He was still many yards from her, as close as the embassy would allow any vehicle. Israel, along with most of its fellow Middle East brethren, had survived centuries of violence and war. They were no stranger to car bombs, and even in America, they kept the general public at a distance, like most of their fellow embassies on the row.

Josh revved the motor. McDonald threw open his door and jumped into the back, taking his contraption with him. The amateur had insisted on coming with him, and Josh could not shake the man, no matter how hard he tried. Now, he was glad he hadn't been able to.

She practically fell into the car as the guards tried to open the gate to run out. Before she even closed the door, Josh hit the gas and off they went, the motion snapping her against the seat.

She was out of breath, her face a hard mask as she stared straight ahead. "How did you know?"

The truth wasn't pleasant and he'd tell her their theories later. "You might be surprised at what I know."

From the corner of his eye he saw her draw a deep breath and hang her head. "I'm in deep, deep trouble, and I'm not exactly sure from whom."

McDonald piped up from behind them. "I have a list of possibilities."

Josh glared at him in the rearview. "Not helpful."

Naomi jerked her head to look around at the man. "Who the hell are you?"

McDonald stuck out a hand. "Call me Mac. That was an amazing escape. I wish I had it on camera."

"You've got to be kidding," Naomi ground out, seeming to say it to Josh rather than McDonald.

"He *did* help you escape. He shut off the electricity to the gate so you didn't get zapped."

She seemed to reevaluate the man for a moment. "Next time open the damn thing for me."

Mac gave a fake salute. "Hopefully there is no next time."

Naomi sank low in the seat and closed her eyes. "I'm dead."

Josh eased his grip, checking the mirror again, but this time to make sure they weren't being followed. "Join the club."

Surprisingly, she snickered, and he wondered what the world was coming to. "Where are you taking me?"

"I have a friend who wants to talk to you."

She stayed silent, probably figuring out who exactly he was talking about. "The only person I will speak to is someone who's going to help me go to ground and stay alive."

"Director Flynn can do that for you," McDonald volunteered.

Josh might still have to kill him.

"Flynn?" Her dusky skin had paled because of her escape,

but now it took on a gray sheen. "No way. I'll end up in worse shape than if my grandfather gets hold of me."

The guards had run halfway down the block before giving up pursuit. Embassy Row was already in his rearview as he took the next turn. "He's not going to hurt you, Naomi. He just wants to talk."

"Are you really that gullible? Is that what he told you? Do you know how long the U.S. has been trying to nab me?"

He actually didn't. "Why are they after you?"

She huffed and began rubbing her ankle.

"He tries anything like that, he'll have to deal with me." Josh wondered if Flynn were using him. He wouldn't put it past the former field agent, but right now, his gut said that wasn't the case. "I swear, he just wants to talk. If we all put our heads together maybe we can figure out what the hell is going on."

"You don't understand. I can't trust him or anyone else now. I need cash, a disguise, and some weapons. I have to go into hiding."

Josh continued to snake around the familiar blocks, moving them farther away from the danger zone. He turned it over and over in his mind, wanting to help her, yet needing to do his job. "You have no idea why someone wanted to detain you?"

"I broke into my grandfather's office and tried to access his files. I was careful, but maybe I set off a silent alarm."

That was unfortunate. "There was a guy upstairs watching your breakout. Not your grandfather. Any ideas?"

She put an elbow on the door and laid her head in her hand. "A nobody."

"I can assure you, if you aid Director Flynn and help us out, we'll create a new identity for you." McDonald was far too chirpy.

"I don't need Flynn for that," Naomi responded.

The rental car responded to his every motion with an ease that he enjoyed. He didn't want to call attention to them and end up with a cop on his tail, but as he took the interstate, he increased their speed.

What would it be like to go into hiding with her? For the two of them to run away and never resurface again? Would she ever be safe? At least he could pretend to be dead to the world, she was still very much alive, and now he had helped her escape.

It would take Mordecai a while to figure out who had been driving the getaway car, but the man was as shrewd as they came, maybe even more so than Flynn. He would consider all the options, see the big picture and the possibilities, no matter how slim the odds. He would know Josh wasn't dead, and then Josh would become a liability to Naomi. No matter what he did, how hard he tried, he might be the one to end up leading Mordecai and the other Kidon assassins to her.

He'd been in tight situations many times in his life, but never had it felt like there was so much on the line.

He punched in Flynn's number on the Bluetooth.

"What are you doing?" she asked, sitting forward and reaching for his hand as if she would disconnect the call.

"You either go to Langley and speak to him, or I'm calling him right now and you'll do it in the car."

She realized she was his prisoner at the moment. The only way to stop him was to create an accident, which she wasn't ready to do. Scooting as far over in the seat as she could, her back half against the door, she looked like a toddler refusing to listen.

Flynn came on. "What's happening?"

"You want to interrogate Naomi? Do it now."

It took half a heartbeat for Flynn to catch on. "You have her?"

"Is she okay?" This from Julia.

McDonald sat forward between the seats. "What an escape. We helped, but she was amazing."

Josh shoved the guy back, and glanced at Naomi before returning his gaze to the road. "Come on, baby girl. This is your chance to let someone help you. You can't do this alone."

"Bullshit."

Okay, he'd expected that.

"Naomi," Flynn said, "I understand your reluctance to talk. Let's call a truce for the next few minutes, and you think it over. I can offer you asylum. I can outsmart your grandfather. I know you have no reason to believe me, and I respect that. I don't trust you either, and if you so much as hurt a hair on either of my operative's heads, I'll come for you. Just so we understand each other."

Josh flicked a concerned gaze her way and saw she was smiling.

God, this woman.

"I like him," she said under her breath to Josh, then to Flynn, "I need a safe place to stay overnight. Think you can handle that?"

There was a pause on Flynn's end, and Josh heard the satisfaction in his boss' voice. "Yeah, I know a spot."

As he rattled off the address, Josh found he was smiling, too.

❄ 15 ❄

W*est Virginia*

THE TWO-STORY AT THE TOP OF THE HILL WAS A SAFE HOUSE not far from the Appalachian Trail. "Flynn and his wife used this place a few years ago," he told Naomi as they wound their way up the gravel drive. "Not many outside Langley's walls know about that little incident. Hell, most inside don't know all the details. Ace told me, that's the only reason I found out."

He thought she'd ask for specifics, but she was lost in her own world. He understood, and left her to it. For now.

She was running on fumes, and he was, too. They both needed a meal, sleep, and time in order to sort out everything that had happened in the past twenty-four hours.

Inside, she slumped on a chair at the kitchen table.

Non-perishable foods were stored in a small pantry, and an assortment of men and women's clothing hung in the closets. A secret room in the basement held a cache of communications equipment. His shoes—still Ace's sneakers—squeaked on the linoleum floor as he found a bottle of Chivas and two shot glasses.

He poured the alcohol, then found a bag of peas in the freezer. Taking her injured foot in hand, he hoisted it to his lap and placed the bag on it. "Drink."

For once she didn't argue. She knocked back the brown liquid, closed her eyes, then poured herself another. That went down quick as a wink and the glass clinked on the tabletop when she set it down. "I'm fucked."

"I'm dead, nice to meet you."

Her tired eyes met his. "I'm serious. I always know the risks going into any op, but this one...this went so far sideways, I have whiplash."

She was gutted over her grandfather, and none of them actually knew exactly what the old guy was up to. No surprise, though. Mordecai may have been a douchebag, but he was still family.

Josh wasn't one for platitudes or positive outlooks. That's not what she needed anyway. "We are far from having all the answers, and if I know anything, even one missing piece of a puzzle can change everything. Tomorrow, we'll start at the beginning. Put everything out on the table. Then we can start eating the elephant one bite at a time."

"Tastes like chicken," she said, totally deadpan.

He grinned. "I believe you have that confused with alligator."

She shivered visibly. "Nasty things."

At least she was trying to find her usual sense of humor. That was a good sign. "Come on. Let's get you in the shower and I'll fix something to eat."

Grabbing the whiskey bottle, she followed him deeper inside the house. "I need to know the makeup of the bomb."

He flicked on the bathroom light, found towels and piled

them on the vanity. "Not sure I can get that, but I'll try. For now, stop thinking about it."

But two hours later, he couldn't sleep and neither could she. Over coffee, they'd discussed the players and the possibilities, but finally, they needed to do more than speculate.

"I want to have a look at the site," Josh said.

"Why?"

"Maybe it will tell me something. After the bombing, I wasn't focused on catching the culprit. I may have overlooked the obvious."

She nodded and stood, keeping her weight on her good foot. Her hair was pulled back in a ponytail and the clothes he'd found for her were loose on her frame, but she was motivated again. "Then let's go."

❧

"I'VE GOT IT."

Julia stormed through the door, holding a set of papers above her head and waving them like a victory flag.

Conrad wasn't surprised. "Don't tell Del you're better than he is at hacking."

She smacked the papers down in front of him, leaned forward and laid a hot one on his lips. Before she could pull away, he grabbed her by the back of the neck and deepened the kiss. It was always a win for him when she was excited about something she'd accomplished.

When they eventually came up for air, she stood back and crossed her arms. Her cheeks were flushed and her eyes snapped with excitement. "I didn't hack into the Bureau's system to get it."

He was slightly disappointed. "You didn't?"

"While I may be *persona non grata* at J. Edgar Hoover, I do still have friends inside the walls. No man is an island, Con. Friends are good."

He *was* an island. She could argue all day about needing friends, but Smitty and Vaughn were it for him. And Julia, of course, but she was so much more than a friend.

He scanned the top page with a brief analysis of the bomb. "So you bribed someone. Do I want to know what you promised them in exchange for his report?"

Disgruntled, she flopped in the chair, hanging her arms over the sides. "Just a Merlot."

He glanced at her, saw her poker face, and knew exactly which one. "You bribed them with a four hundred dollar bottle of wine that I specifically brought from Rome for you?"

She gave him a charming smile and a cute shrug. "You don't even like wine, and although I had some pretty impressive plans for it, this is more important."

He thumbed through the next two sheets, looking for the information that he wanted. "I'll get you a new bottle."

"I'll go with you to pick it up."

He liked that idea, his attention scanning the FBI's potential suspects based on the profiler's analysis of the bomb site. He noticed that below the three names listed, each connected to a terrorist organization. But someone—a particular spy he slept with—had hand-printed a fourth.

Julia was an expert on bombs and their makers. He sat back and smiled. "You added the last name on the list."

She had that look on her face, telling him she was on the trail of something important. "Rahab. Disappeared approximately two years ago."

"Is that the first or last name?"

"The only. Like Cher or Prince."

Seemed vaguely familiar, but he didn't have every terrorist

in the world logged in his memory. "Why doesn't the Bureau suspect him?"

She shot forward, bracing her hands on her knees. "Scuttlebutt on the dark web suggests he was murdered, but there's no proof he's even dead."

"You don't think he is."

"For a period of ten years throughout Western Europe and the Middle East, an unknown assailant destroyed multiple corporate offices and research centers. He was never identified, no photos, no trail. A ghost that was whispered about between intelligence agencies and the black market. I'm reviewing a list of those bombings and fires, but what if Rahab went dark and spread the rumor about his own death?"

"Why surface now?"

"Like with any criminal who seems to take a vacation for a while, he could have been in prison or recovering from an injury or illness. Most agencies chalked off those bombings to arsonists, anarchists, corporate warfare, and because they weren't government-related, never pursued other angles. Those of us who know bombs found the puzzle fascinating. In looking at the bigger picture and considering the improbable as well as impossible, my gut says Rahab may have played a part in this, or even groomed someone for the job."

Potential suspects were then numerous, especially if there was no identification or photo of this particular bomber. "Rahab had to be backed by someone, or had a connection to the players involved. He could've been in this country for the past two years working for DeValdi for all we know."

Julia nodded. "I have at least seven more bombings to review that are potentially linked to him, but I already read about one where they believe he was acting as a janitor. He had access to the building after hours, as well as the chemicals necessary to create the explosion."

"We've been running background checks on DeValdi's

employees, but it looks like we better extend that to contracted ones as well."

She stood and leaned on the desk again. "We need to keep this hush-hush. If Rahab believes he's invisible to everyone, maybe he'll make a mistake and we can catch him. The community at large believes he's dead, and on the surface this does look like a simple corporate sabotage."

The lie to the public had been that the senator and the others were taking a tour of DeValdi's institution, keeping Project Disruption under wraps. "If I were Rahab, I'd already have fled the country, wouldn't you?"

She worried her bottom lip, considering it. "Not necessarily. Everybody believes he's dead and buried, so no one's looking for him. He may have crawled back into his hole, but if he's coming out of retirement, we may be able to catch him."

"You didn't share this with your friend at the Bureau, did you?"

She grinned. "The profilers there are quite full of themselves, and for good reason, but no, I kept this little nugget just for you."

He stood and went around the desk, grabbing her and pulling her close. "As soon as this is done, we'll head to Rome for that bottle of wine."

She kissed him and laughed. "And maybe make a pit stop in Paris?"

He would give her anything she wanted to see the smile that she was offering now. "I've wanted to take you back there for a long time."

She smacked him on the ass. "Just so you know, I'm taking that as a promise, and you're not getting out of it."

He acted hurt that she would think he would try such a thing. She grinned, sashayed to the door, and blew him a kiss before exiting.

❧ 16 ❧

D*e Valdi Industries*

THE BOMB SITE WAS EVEN MORE HAZARDOUS IN THE MIDDLE of the night. The nearby solar lights had been destroyed, and the assorted businesses evacuated, the streets around the area pitch black.

No one was allowed in or out, but there was also minor security keeping an eye on the place now. Naomi followed Josh on a circuitous route through various piles of debris, feeling odd. She had no home at the moment, and was relying on American spies to keep her safe.

I can keep myself safe.

At least she hoped she could.

He led her to the general area the FBI and CIA believed was ground zero. She wasn't sure what the two of them could uncover that investigators had not, but she understood his need to go back to the scene and recreate it in his mind. It was always possible that those collecting what fragments they could identify from the detonation had missed something, but without knowing for sure what they were looking for, she doubted she and Josh would have better luck.

The smell was still what got her, a combination of death and destruction she normally wasn't exposed to in her line of work. Poisoning was simpler, less messy, except for the person who ingested it. Bombing was so...cowardly, in her opinion. Too many others ended up paying the price and the target became simply another face in the crowd. At least when she struck, they knew who and why they'd been targeted. There were no casualties of war.

Except for Rahab.

She'd actually killed fewer people than Josh suspected, she was sure. Many times, her job involved making someone sick enough that they missed a critical meeting or at least, understood it was a warning. That next time if they stepped over the line, it would be fatal. She could hold a gun to anyone's head, but she'd found threatening their loved ones with a long painful poisoning was often more effective in blackmail.

Every target had a weak spot. She'd become good at her work by knowing it.

Josh stopped, his shadowed form kneeling to push rubble away. His flashlight caught on metal rods that had most likely been part of the building's internal structure.

Naomi gingerly stepped to his side, her ankle throbbing. "What is it?"

He pulled up a piece of yellow plastic that looked like it had come from a commercial mop bucket. "Nothing," he said, flipping it away.

Her gaze followed the trajectory of it. The sight of it jogged her memory, but it was gone a second later when he rose and let out a frustrated curse. "This is pointless."

Maybe for the reasons he was thinking, but not completely. "Do you want to keep looking?"

He turned in a circle, carefully scanning the area. There had been people buried under layers of concrete, complete floors above them falling on them like a crushing monster. She knew their deaths would weigh heavily on him.

They did on her, too, for a reason she couldn't quite explain. She'd been so honed in on her own issues, and trying to steal Disruption while setting Josh up for it, she'd never dreamed another person could sneak in and destroy all of this. If she had been more cautious, more detached, and focused, she wouldn't have missed the bomber.

She worked her way over to the plastic, studying it. It wasn't like she carried a dossier of every terrorist in her head, and the best of them often changed their appearance through temporary, or even permanent, means. Still, there was a nagging sense that she had overlooked something—something important.

While both of them had their phone ringers off, she saw Josh reach in to his back pocket when his vibrated. He pulled it out, frowning at whatever message had come through. Finding his footing as he made his way over to her, he held it out to show her the screen. "Does this mean anything to you?"

Her blood ran cold, the word on the screen sending an echo through her mind. She took a step back, instinctively. "What about it?"

"Flynn wants to know if you recognize the name?"

Why was he asking about a dead assassin? "I've heard it," she said, noncommittal.

"And? That's it?"

She turned and headed toward the car, her injured ankle screaming at her when a chunk of concrete shifted and she twisted it. She heard Josh curse and begin following.

Neither of them said anything until they were inside the car. He didn't start the engine, but faced her. "You obviously know more about Rahab than you're saying. Is it some kind of message?"

It was a message all right, she just wasn't sure exactly how it was possible. "What does Flynn want to know? The term can mean chaos monster, or it can refer to several different historical entities."

The text was still visible and Josh stared at it. "It must have something to do with this. Is this a person's name? Like our bomber's?"

She shook her head, refusing to look at him. "It can't be."

"What?"

"Rahab is dead."

Josh tossed the phone on the dash and started the engine. "This Rahab is a terrorist?"

"Was."

"Maybe he's like me, dead but not dead, you know?"

As he pulled away from the curb, she gripped the seat. Her balance was off, her mind whirling. The memory of her grandfather's calendar flashed through her brain. "That's not possible, and by the way, Rahab was a woman."

"Anything's possible, Naomi."

Her stomach churned. "Not this."

He glanced at her, back to the road. "How do you know?"

"Because..." She swallowed past her uncertainty. Assassins didn't give up their secrets, but she'd left that life behind now, hadn't she? "I killed her."

❧ 17 ❧

W*est Virginia*

No matter what he asked, he couldn't get Naomi to talk again until they were back at the farmhouse. He could tell her ankle was killing her, and he guided her to the sofa, propping it on the coffee table, while he went to create another makeshift ice bag.

He returned with the remaining whiskey, glasses, and repeated what he'd done earlier, this time pulling her foot on top of his lap after handing her a double shot of alcohol.

He wanted to push, demand, interrogate her. That would be folly.

She leaned against lime green pillows, allowing him to massage her leg and foot, occasional tiny moans escaping from her lips. All was quiet except for those sounds that climbed under his skin and turned his thoughts to their lovemaking.

His fantasies wove around him, Mr. Happy urging him to

take her right there on the couch, but that was also folly. She was in no mood for sex, no mood for anything, it seemed.

"Rahab is the emblematic name of Egypt," she said quietly. "It also refers to rage, fierceness, insolence, and pride."

He slowed his fingers, waiting for her to go on. She looked at him from half-lidded eyes. "The term is used in both the Old and New Testaments. At times, as I mentioned previously, it refers to a chaotic monster, and it can be from the sea. Some believe it refers to the void, where all creation was chaos before God came along and conquered it."

While his Catholic upbringing had been forced upon him, Josh didn't know much about biblical text. However, if she was talking, he was ready to listen all night.

"It's also the name of a woman, possibly a prostitute or an innkeeper who helped the Israelites in Jericho." Naomi sipped her whiskey. "She hid two spies who were sent to scout the city prior to an attack. They stayed in her house, which was built into the city wall. She was able to help them escape the soldiers who were sent to capture them, and the spies promised to spare her and her family when the city was taken. She was clever, tricky, and unafraid to disobey and deceive her king. Her allegiance was to God and Israel, something my grandfather drilled in to me."

Josh's hands stilled on her calf. "Why did you kill her? The modern day version?"

"That wasn't my assignment, but she managed to get in the way. It was really nothing more than an accident, or maybe fate. The original Rahab may have been saved by spies, but the namesake who *was* a spy, apparently didn't receive God's grace."

He could feel her weariness seeping into his own bones. It was well after midnight and they both needed sleep. Neither of their brains were at top form, but in the dark of the room, a singular lamp glowing yellow on the side table, he eased down slightly and started rubbing her leg again. "Is there any way that she survived? That she's behind DeValdi's attack?"

Naomi closed her eyes and didn't answer for a long moment. Her breathing was normal, her body relaxed, and he wondered for a heartbeat if she'd fallen asleep. She cracked open one eye, closed it again, and sighed deeply. "Like you said, anything's possible."

"Do you think she had some tie to Dr. DeValdi, or anyone involved in Project Disruption?"

Slowly and stiffly, Naomi pushed off the pillows, removing her leg from his lap. She downed the last of the drink and set the glass on the coffee table. "I haven't thought about her in a long time. I have no idea, but it doesn't seem her style to go do something like this on her own. She was hired, and we have to identify by who, if we're going to figure out the why."

She leaned forward to put her head in her hands, defeat sagging her body. Along with the message about Rahab, Flynn's follow-up texts had been about the fact that members of the Israeli Embassy, including Mordecai, had been searching for her all over D.C. Not just her, of course, because as Josh suspected, Mordecai wasn't convinced he was dead.

The old bastard was too smart for his own good, and underlying everything, Josh was determined to keep Naomi safe.

He reached over to rub her back and felt a modicum of tension leave her shoulders. "I know things have gone to shit for you, but whatever you decide to do about your future, I'll back you on it."

The look she turned on him took his breath away, as if she couldn't quite understand why he would risk his future for hers. "Did you ever bring Emily here?"

The sudden change in subject left him at a loss. "Emily?"

Her eyes were unforgiving as they bore holes into him. "Is that her cover name? The woman you were in Cairo with, the weekend fling that turned into a relationship last year."

And oh boy, he was glad she didn't have any poison on her at the moment, because she looked like a venomous snake ready to strike if he said the wrong thing. Except, he wasn't sure exactly what *was* the right thing to say. All he could do was tell her the truth. "Her real name is Libby, and she's a counterterrorism analyst that Flynn paired me with for an assignment. There was no relationship. We had to act as husband and wife, that's all, and how do you even know about her? Were you following me?"

"Me? No. My grandfather, however, made you his business after he found out about us." Her thumb tapped against her leg. Nerves? "He told me—"

"He told you wrong." Did she even get nervous? He'd never asked. "Did you ever consider he was trying to drive a wedge between us?"

"So you never brought her to your place."

Irritation burned under his skin. "No, I've never brought her, or anyone else, to the apartment. I don't have relationships, Naomi." *Outside of you.* "They get in the way, as you well know."

She tried to cover her relief by turning away and reaching for her drink, but he caught her wrist and forced her to face him again. "You're the only one that I've ever become attached to since I joined the Agency. Some operative I am, huh? Falling for an assassin."

It was meant as a joke, but she jerked her wrist from his grip and looked like she was trying to decide whether to spit in his face or kiss him.

He grinned, daring her to do the latter.

Lucky for him, she took the bait. Her fingers dove into

his hair, jerking him forward so her lips met his. It was so sudden and violent, their teeth clunked together.

Hell if he cared.

Her mouth ravaged his, as if she couldn't get enough of him. As if she needed to absolve herself of something. He understood that feeling, that need. Everything flew out of his brain, and he lifted her onto his lap.

He tugged off her shirt, and she went to work unbuttoning his, growing frustrated and ripping the last few off in her haste. It was like they'd never been together, like two teenagers caught up in a fierce lust in the backseat of a car. Her tongue jammed into his mouth as she pushed his shoulders against the couch and went to work on his pants.

Grabbing her hips, he twisted and laid her down under him, then removed hers slowly and carefully. She watched him with hooded eyes, her desire burning brightly in them. Once done with that, he trailed his fingers over her bare thighs and she gripped his pants, tugging at the zipper.

Standing, he undid them the rest of the way and let them fall to the ground. She wasn't wearing underwear tonight, and she spread her legs wide for him.

So beautiful. He ached to enter her and drive away her demons. She was the drug that could drive his away as well. The world could take a flying fuck—he didn't care about anything or anyone but her.

Slowing himself down, he lowered his lips between her legs and enjoyed the feast in front of him. She bucked and arched under his ministrations, her fingernails digging into his hair, his skull.

The moans he loved echoed in the room. He thumbed her sensitive spot as his tongue drove deep inside her, over and over. She panted and begged. Pleaded.

Just the way he liked it.

More than once, she attempted to tug his mouth away to

keep her climax at bay. He knew what she wanted—full-on body slamming sex—and he was going to enjoy plunging into her depths, but for now, he had one mission—to drive out all doubts about him and his obsession with her.

Her and only her.

Talking about relationships was torture, but he could show her how he felt. He wanted to make love to each and every part of her body. Blot out the ugly memories, the lies and half-truths she'd lived under. Mordecai couldn't have her anymore—she belonged to him.

As he brought her to the brink, he mentally promised to never lie to her again. She cried out his name, along with something in her native tongue, her body arching so hard, he held her hips to anchor her. She rode the orgasm, and he continued sucking at her delicate, swollen flesh, teasing it until she whimpered for mercy.

Boneless, she lay in a blissful stupor. Pleased, he slowly made his way back up her body, licking the skin above her pubis, stopping at her belly button to nibble the sensitive skin, and kissing each of her ribs in turn. He gorged on her beautiful breasts, her groans turning into tight needy mews. With his tongue, he flicked at her nipples, then sucked each deep into his mouth.

Her hand found his erection and squeezed. She began a rhythm that had him gasping for air and he caught her bottom lip between his teeth. Tightening her grip, she stared into his eyes, daring him to deny her a turn in the game. In response, he released her lip, bucking into her hand.

She kissed his neck, murmured encouragement in his ear, and sucked on the lobe, as her nimble grip controlled him, building a rhythm he couldn't deny. He was nearly gone when she guided him inside her hot, slick folds, and locked her legs around his hips.

They fit together perfectly. Like always, the fire that

burned in their veins, fueling their passion, blazed between them. She was so competitive she tried to make him come before she would let herself go, but not tonight. He knew how to hang on, how to tease and manipulate her into climaxing first.

Plus, as he'd be happy to remind her later, he'd already won that race.

Her nails dug into his back, trailing down to his ass cheeks and encouraging him to pump faster, harder. He pulled her commanding hands away, pinning them over her head to the pillow. "Come for me, baby girl," he murmured against her lips. "You're mine tonight. Let me have it all."

She shattered beneath him, crying out to God and Allah, and cursing him in the next breath. He laughed, loving his control over her, but in the next moment, she broke free from his restraint, grabbed him again, and arched, creating a different kind of tension. Her muscles closed around him, so tight, so perfect. "You're mine," she countered. "Don't make me kill you."

His vision went white, and the next thing he knew, he was falling.

Falling into her, falling into...

Love.

If his brain cells had been working, it would have scared the shit out of him, but at that moment, he didn't care. He let himself die in the ecstasy of her words, her body. Hell, he egged himself on. The two of them were a train wreck, the chaos Rahab was named for.

Whatever came in the next few days, they would handle it together, and as Josh pulled Naomi against him in the aftermath of another shared orgasm, he vowed that no one had better get in their way.

＊ 18 ＊

Naomi was tired and sore, aching in all the right places, along with her still swollen ankle, but happy as she poured cereal into two bowls at the counter the next morning.

The lower leg was black and blue and probably needed a soft cast. She hadn't broken it, but definitely injured some tendons or ligaments. Josh had insisted she prop it on a pillow all night, but between their lovemaking and her need to sleep curled up next to him, the pillow ended up on the floor repeatedly.

What was she doing? Had she seriously just turned her amazing life as a Kidon assassin into a flaming ball of disaster?

That thought brought up dozens of others that left her shaky. Had her grandfather lied to her about Josh and Emily on purpose? What else had he lied about?

A tear slid down her cheek and she dashed it away. He was all she had left for family, and now, she couldn't even look him in the face.

What would have happened if the embassy guards had

apprehended her? Would she still be in one of the cold, harsh interrogation rooms, pleading for her life? Would he truly have her—his granddaughter—killed if she defied him?

Josh walked up behind her, sneaking his hands under the shirt she wore—the one he'd been in last night, missing buttons and all—and pinned her against the cabinet. She smiled down into the bowls. It was the first time she could remember feeling like this, her world turned upside down, and yet...this felt right.

He kissed the back of her neck, shifting her hair out of the way so he could nuzzle her ear. She gave in and let him, looping an arm around his neck and enjoying the feel of his strong body pressing against hers.

He was still a jerk, gloating in her ear, "How many times was that? Six? Ten? I believe I'm way ahead of you in the race."

She smacked his ear, and he yelped, jumping back. Facing him, the tails of the shirt rustled against her thighs. She grinned. "Extenuating circumstances, and I get a pass on every one of those."

"A pass? Why?"

"I'm injured and I've been through hell the past few days."

"Using the old I'm hurt card." He made wah-wah noises and rubbed his fists in his eyes to mimic crying. "Some tough Mossad agent you are."

She tried to punch him but he dodged out of the way, his bare chest mesmerizing in the morning light. He danced on his feet and impersonated a boxer, circling around her and throwing fake punches in the air. "You think you can take me, assassin? Put up your dukes."

For the first time in months, she laughed. This was her favorite part of their relationship. The sex was amazing, but this? The teasing, wise cracks, and banter—she lived for this. It was their version of a secret pact, an allegiance of sorts. It was all theirs and the heavy weight she'd lived under all her life lightened when Josh was around.

Which made no sense. He'd caused the death of her career, the loss of her grandfather.

"I could take you with one hand behind my back and my injured ankle."

"Is that so?"

She flashed him a boob.

He stopped dancing, lowered his fists, looking completely awe-struck. "Damn."

"Exactly."

The smile he flashed her was mischievous, evil, as she covered herself again. "This is the first time I've ever actually seen you the morning after. Usually you escape before sunrise."

She handed him a bowl and spoon. "You're going to need fuel for today, but there's no milk."

He accepted it and snagged a cup of coffee, placing both on the table. "I think maybe we should lay low, regroup. I need to strategize with Flynn before we do anything else."

"Your handler has been calling and texting you." She pointed at the burner phone on the counter. "I think he's about to pee his pants, thinking that I've killed you for real this time."

Josh flipped through the messages as Naomi crunched a mouthful of dry cereal, pouring her own coffee. "You read these?"

"Only the first two or three." She winked at him. "After that it was the same, 'where are you,' 'what are you doing' garbage. He's worried. It's cute."

Josh sighed. "It's his first assignment. What a way to break him in, huh? Not only is it a domestic operation, which he can never admit to, but it involves me."

"The worst," she agreed with a dramatic roll of her eyes.

She raked her fingers through her hair, taking a seat at the table. "Sink or swim, yes?"

Josh joined her, setting the phone down and inhaling half his coffee. Then he looked up, catching sight of something outside. She heard an alarm go off deep in the house, connected to the security system.

She shot to her feet, the comfortable morning forgotten in the pounding of her heart. She should have known better than to let her guard down!

He also stood, but motioned her to relax. "Friends, not enemies. You might want to put some actual clothes on, though."

As her attention went to the car coming up the drive, she realized he was right. It wasn't an approaching enemy, but nevertheless, could be at any moment. She wasn't about to face Flynn and whoever else was with him while wearing nothing but Josh's shirt.

The safe house had a variety of clothes and sizes. Although it was summer and would hit the nineties again today, she layered a linen shirt over a tank top and found a pair of stretchy pants that hugged her curves.

Josh greeted their visitors and she slipped into the bathroom. Her hair was still damp from her shower but starting to frizz. She ran a brush through it, tugged it into a high ponytail, and wrapped her ankle with a stretchy sports bandage she found in the cabinet.

The sound of voices in the kitchen made her antsy. It had been nice for the few hours she and Josh had been able to ignore the world, forget about their problems, and escape in each other, but now reality was crashing back down on them, and she knew what she had to do.

Putting on her detached face, she entered the kitchen and was introduced to a striking brunette who smiled at her and shook her hand. "Julia Torrison. Nice to finally meet you," she said. "I've heard a lot about you."

Naomi knew a few things about her as well, but decided she'd keep that to herself. "I appreciate your cooperation," she told Flynn. Very few men or women ever intimidated her, but after being in Russia, helping Josh with a mission to rescue a lost princess, she'd discovered Flynn was a formidable opponent. One she didn't want to cross.

He set a folder on the kitchen table and flipped the cover open. "I know this photo is blurry, but have you ever seen this woman before?"

Naomi stared at it, the subject's profile obscured by a ball cap and the collar of a work uniform turned up around her neck. "I can't make a positive identification, no. Why?"

Julia helped herself to coffee. "Could be our bomber. We have a strong suspicion that whoever it was started working for a contractor that DeValdi hired three months ago. I know you're familiar with Rahab, and we're wondering if there's any other information you can provide that can help us locate her."

"I've seen her up close and personal, but I couldn't recognize my own mother in that picture. Didn't she have a photo ID on file with the contractor?"

Conrad tapped the table, his fingers denoting his impatience, or possibly annoyance. "Someone wiped the files. All of them, not just this employee's. The only reason we flagged her is because she went to work for them two weeks after DeValdi hired this service."

"What type of contractor?" Josh asked.

"Janitorial," Torrison supplied.

Naomi saw a light come on in Josh's eyes as he glanced at her. "The mop bucket."

Flynn stopped tapping. "What?"

"At ground zero," he answered. "There were shards of a

commercial mop bucket—one of those bright yellow ones—in the rubble. It seemed odd amongst all the other wreckage in the center of the blast sight."

Torrison nodded at Flynn. "Same as the Vanguard explosion in London five years ago."

London. Something tickled at Naomi's brain. "Vanguard Importers?"

Torrison's sharp gaze turned to her. "Yes, you know them? Know about the bombing?"

"It was the last job Rahab completed before..." She hesitated, her training kicking in and keeping her from divulging information in this new, untested alliance.

"Before you killed her," Josh finished, and then added for Flynn and Torrison's benefit, "accidently."

"You killed Rahab?" Torrison seemed incredulous; Flynn not so much.

"She wasn't my target. She simply got in the way."

Torrison made a "hunh" noise. Flynn scrutinized her, doubt clearly evident in his features. "Sloppy on your part or hers?"

Naomi bristled, but he was calling it like he saw it. "Both."

"She used you to fake her own death." Torrison now seemed impressed. "I wouldn't call that sloppy. I'd call it smart."

"You knew her personally?" Flynn asked.

"We weren't friends, if that's what you're asking. She was an extremely secretive person. She kept the lowest profile of anyone I've ever known in intelligence and security. Few have ever seen her or spoken to her. It's what made her perfect for her job—you can't catch a ghost who has no connections, no friends, no identity."

"No man is an island," Flynn stated with a derisive snort. "But maybe a few are."

This seemed to be pointed at Torrison who rolled her

eyes. "Why did she want the world to believe she was dead, if she was already impossible to trace or apprehend?"

Good question. "Off the top of my head? Two possibilities," Naomi told her. "She wanted out of the terrorist game, or someone paid her to stop."

A pregnant silence fell as all three of them turned that over.

"Why would she want out?" Josh asked.

An even better question.

"She was losing her edge," Flynn offered.

"She was blackmailed," Torrison added.

Naomi looked at Josh, a warm sensation in her chest. "She fell in love."

He met her eyes. His fingers grazed across the back of her hand.

Did he feel it, too? This tug, drawing her to him like he was her true north?

"So she staged her death, curtesy of the best assassin out there." Flynn caught Naomi's eye. "Why come out of retirement now?"

Josh listed the common motivators: "Money. Revenge. Blackmail."

"Power," Naomi supplied. "This whole thing has been about power and who controls it." At Flynn's look, she went on, deciding it was time to lay everything on the table. "Israel is concerned about the U.S. gaining too much power using a weapon like Disruption. I was supposed to steal the technology and frame Josh for it, making it look as though he sold it to the Brits, when in reality, Israel could then use it secretively if necessary to control both allies."

All were silent for a tense few ticks of the clock, then Flynn glanced at Josh. "You sure know how to pick 'em."

Torrison elbowed him. "Con..." Her tone was a warning.

Naomi looked at the floor. "No, he's right. I'm not

someone you'd take home to mommy." Her gaze rose. "I've done things for my country I'm not proud of, but they were all done in the name of freedom and the common good. I'm sure you can say the same about your missions."

Flynn blew out a breath. "No one's passing judgment, least of all me. I've been in your shoes, and I know how tough those calls can be when it's between your assignment and your conscious. All I'm saying to my operative"—he shot Josh a stern look—"is that he's let his dick get him into a dire predicament."

Josh raised his hands in a surrender gesture. "It's true. We can all agree I'm an idiot and I let my country down by falling for Naomi. Moving on..."

Torrison tried to hide a grin. Josh reached for Naomi's hand.

She took it. "I don't know if this has anything to do with Rahab, but a Brit named Colin Barber has been hanging around the embassy, supposedly working on a culture exchange between Israel and Britain this fall. Some kind of technology scholarship for women. He's MI5 and his real name is Henry Adamson."

Torrison and Flynn exchanged a look. "Truman," they said in unison.

Flynn withdrew his phone and dialed. Torrison filled her in. "Truman Gunn is a friend, also in British Intelligence. He might know this Adamson."

While Flynn left a message, Naomi studied the picture again, but her focus was on Josh. He wanted this to be the attacker. He needed a target to track down, to lash out at and exact revenge, and she wanted to give that to him more than anything.

Problem was, she couldn't.

"I need to confront my grandfather," she told them when Flynn hung up. Their friend was unavailable right then. "I can get information from him regarding Rahab, if she *is* still alive."

Both Josh and Flynn chorused their disagreement. "No way in hell," Josh said.

"I'm sorry, Naomi." Flynn pocketed his phone and closed the folder. "That would be suicide. He may be your grandfather, but I wouldn't trust him."

The fact she shouldn't either was left unsaid, but still hung in the air. What she'd realized this morning in the peace and quiet of the farmhouse was that he was the missing piece. She was sure, without a doubt, that behind all of this, he was the person who could tie the threads together.

A person who craved power like ducks needed water.

"He won't kill me—and believe it or not, I'm not stupid. I'll go in, be contrite, tell him whatever he wants to hear. It's not like I haven't manipulated him before."

She put on her cold, detached face, acting as if she wasn't shaking under it at the thought of confronting Mordecai.

Flynn didn't buy it. "Sorry, but I can't allow you to do that. I have too much blood on my hands at the moment, and so does Josh. We should've seen this coming, should've been prepared, and we weren't. I'm not taking any more chances, and I'm sure as hell not letting you go back to the embassy after your incident yesterday."

She leaned a hip on the table, trying to look calm and in control. "Come on, Director. You know I can handle myself, and the smart move here is to use me as bait. I'm probably the only person who can get him to confess, if he had his fingers anywhere near this. And if he didn't? So be it. We cross him off the list and move on."

Josh was adamantly shaking his head no. "I'm with Flynn. It would be suicide. I know you want to believe the best of the old guy, but once you go in there, I—*we*—can't protect you."

She put up a decent fight for another five minutes, then reluctantly agreed with Flynn's plan. She didn't want to make it obvious that she was pulling one over on them, and when he insisted on moving her and Josh to a new, even safer locale, she again put up a protest.

It was only enough to make them all believe she was actually standing her ground. Eventually, she gave in, excusing herself to go to the bathroom. On her way, she grabbed Josh's backpack.

She'd checked all the escape routes last night, and sneaking out the bathroom window was a piece of cake. Stuffing the bag with a few essential items, she pulled on her shoes, ignoring the pain in her ankle, and opened the lower casement.

Josh would see it as betrayal. He'd come after her. She couldn't blame him—if the situation were flipped, she'd be mad as hell that he ran away, and she'd make him pay for it when she caught him.

She smiled to herself as she quietly removed the screen and let it fall to the ground outside. What would that reunion be like? Hot and passionate, she guessed, just like all their meetings, whether they were mad or simply in need of the other's presence to help them get through the night.

She had to be careful so she didn't land on her ankle, and she debated whether to go out with her left leg first or the right. When he realized she was gone, he'd know she was headed for the embassy and her grandfather, and he could move a lot faster than she could. The smart thing would be to disable the vehicles or steal one of them, but it would be too obvious. She would have to hitchhike into the city without getting caught. Even if they staked out the embassy, she could contact her grandfather and have him meet her somewhere else, somewhere that let her control what happened.

She was so busy thinking about her plans, she didn't see

the shadow at the corner of the house until after she'd landed on her butt. The shock of her ankle smacking against the wooden back porch made her grunt.

"You never fail to disappoint." Josh leaned on the wooden siding, not even offering to help her up. "Going somewhere?"

❧ 19 ❧

Conrad had even more respect for Naomi after she tried to escape. He was also proud of his operative for knowing she would.

As he and Julia stood in the kitchen, listening to the argument going on in the bedroom, Julia nudged him with her shoulder as they leaned against the counter. "She's an initiator."

He wasn't sure if he was glad for Julia's obsession with the new psychological definitions she was using to evaluate everyone these days, but she was never off the mark. Stone's wife, Dr. Brigit Kent, had developed these profiling attributes as an offshoot of the Meyers-Brigg psychology test that the CIA had used for decades. The good doctor, a contractor for Homeland, had become close friends with his wife. The two of them spent hours analyzing people and situations for fun.

Fun. He could think of better things to do with Julia's time. "Well, she's gonna be a dead initiator if she doesn't stop being so bullheaded."

"There's the pot-kettle statement we know and love." She grinned at the face he made. "I tried to get Brigit to use bullheaded for one of the labels, because heaven knows I've had to put up with it with you, but she didn't think it was appropriate. Can you believe that?"

She nudged him again, this time with her elbow right in his ribs. He kissed her cheek, but he couldn't drum up his normal return banter. Things were serious and shit was about to hit the fan. He turned to lean on the sink, staring out the window. *Ace should be here with the hearse by now.*

Naomi stomped out of the bedroom and into the kitchen. At least she tried. It was more of a stomp-hop-stomp. Her injured ankle kept giving out on her, causing her to wince in pain. "You can't hold me against my will."

Josh sauntered in behind her, a ghost of a smile on his lips as he peered at Conrad over her head. "Think she should see a doctor?"

He doubted she'd let a physician look at her. "Believe me, Naomi, if I had a choice, I'd be happy to drop you at the closest bus station and say good luck. Let you figure out how to get yourself out of our country. But Homeland is now watching your grandfather, and they're looking for you, too. How far do you think you'd get?"

Her chin rose. "I have skills and resources you can't imagine."

Bluff and bravado. "The biggest reason I'm trying to help you is because this is about more than just you and Mordecai. My operative is involved, and my loyalty lies with him. The two of you have screwed up with your relationship, and now it's reflecting on *my* job." His cell went off and he glanced at the screen. Ace's text told him he was turning up the drive and not to shoot him. He pocketed the phone, and readied himself for another argument with Naomi. "You don't get to call the shots," he preempted her next smart-mouthed response. "I do. You may have been an outstanding agent, and I get that you have extreme skills, but that's not enough.

Neither is your bullheadedness. At the end of the day, you're looking at the only people in this country, maybe the entire world, who will help you right now. Are you seriously going to let your pride throw that away?"

The chin stayed in the air. Josh looked at the floor. Conrad could tell he was dying to reach out and touch her, show solidarity, but he was smart enough to know his boss was right.

Julia cleared her throat, giving him a pointed look. He blew out an exasperated sigh. "Look, I'd prefer we did this with respect and a mutually-beneficial alliance between us, but if you choose to make this hard, it's going to get really nasty for you. That injured ankle and your current wanted status on Homeland's radar is the least of your worries."

He'd hit the truth, and it showed on her face. He saw her bite the inside of her cheek, trying to figure out a way to save face. "Where are you taking us?"

"It's a secret compound," Julia said. "We can't let you see where we're going, or tell you the location."

"We'll be safe," Josh added, moving to her side. His knuckles brushed hers. "You're going to have trust someone."

She stayed rigid. Julia took a step toward both of them. "I know it goes against everything you've been trained to believe, by trusting us, but we have your best interests at heart. If you care about Josh, you'll stop fighting us, and work with us to figure out what's going on."

The hearse arrived and Naomi's attention went to the window. "Fine. If Josh trusts you, so will I."

A breakthrough. Finally. Conrad motioned to the front door. They'd already been here longer than he'd planned. "Let's go."

Josh collected their items and hefted his backpack on his shoulder. Outside, Ace opened the back of the hearse. "Yo, I'm Ace, also known as the wheelman." He waved a hand at the contents of the vehicle. "These ain't the finest I have in my line, but they *are* custom."

Naomi went pale. She looked at Conrad with a mixture of fear and disbelief. "You can't be serious."

He tapped his knuckles on the end of one. "They're bulletproof. Just in case."

"Just in case what?"

"We have to consider all angles," Julia assured her. "If by chance we were to be attacked between here and the next location, these will protect you."

"That, and my awesome driving skills," Ace added, touching his chest with his hand.

"What she really means is I'm extremely paranoid and score high as a *futuristic thinker*." He made air quotes around the term. "Supposedly, that means I'm always planning ahead and considering every risk, along with its potential outcome."

Josh touched Naomi's hand. "We prepare for every scenario so we don't get caught off guard. Occasionally, it doesn't work, like with DeValdi, but it's our best weapon— being prepared."

She scanned the landscape, then narrowed her eyes as she stared at the coffins. Conrad could tell her own mortality was what she feared more than climbing inside the box.

He was anxious to get going, but this was the make or break point with her. She was either going to put her faith in them and get in, or she was going to run screaming in the other direction.

With a slow, deliberate exhale, she gave him a nod. Josh took her hand and helped her inside.

20

How many hearses could fit two full-size caskets in them? These sat side-by-side, an eerie sight that made Josh shudder. It was like a bad omen and he didn't even believe in such things.

Naomi must have sensed the same. He was surprised when she insisted he share one with her, but he found he wasn't at all opposed to doing so. He didn't ask her why, only nodded and climbed in with her before Flynn closed the lid on them.

Oxygen was piped in and a two-way radio connected them to the driver. The amount of darkness, however, compounded the sensation of being buried alive.

Once the engine started and they began to move, Naomi said quietly, "I hate enclosed spaces."

A claustrophobic agent? It wasn't unheard of, but the fear was considered a foible. He wondered if she'd ever admitted it to anyone. "No one likes climbing into a coffin when they're still alive."

Her fingers dug into his arm, the two of them spooning in the tight space. The satin pillow under his cheek was cool, and he smelled the soap she'd used that morning. He honestly felt like laughing. They were in a casket for fuck's sake, taking a hearse to an unknown location. This was some real James Bond shit, and his adrenaline was pumping hard.

She squirmed. "Do you know where they're taking us?"

Being pinned against her body made Mr. Happy excited. Her delectable derriere was nestled tight against his cock, and his brain shorted out, thinking about distracting her by sending his fingers down the front of her pants and...

Jesus, he needed her to slap him upside the head. Reminding himself about the gravity of their situation, he forced his brain to refocus. "I'd tell you if I did. There's The Farm, with its training facilities that include safe house structures, interrogation rooms, etc., but also plenty of government buildings and private properties Flynn could be stashing us at."

He didn't know if that appeased her or not, her silence falling like a heavy weight between them. He wasn't surprised she'd tried to run, nor that she'd given in to Flynn. Something in his chest shifted, remembering her expression when Flynn put the guilt on her about placing him in danger. Josh wanted to hate his boss, but he'd seen the truth in Flynn's face. He wasn't using that guilt to merely manipulate her; he was truly concerned about both of them.

The hearse sped up, and they took a sharp left. Naomi's grip on his arm tightened even more. The wheels squealed and they took another abrupt turn.

"What's happening?" Her voice was low and anxious.

"Must be Flynn driving," he told her. "Regardless of his self-assigned 'wheelman' label, Ace doesn't go over fifty miles an hour, and he certainly doesn't take corners like this."

They accelerated again, and Josh suspected they were passing a vehicle. Perfectly normal, he assured himself.

They bumped over something in the road, the rear end fishtailing. *Not as normal.*

His fingers fumbled for the communication device, but he couldn't see anything, and when he started punching buttons, he got no response. "Hey, what's going on up there?"

Only static came back.

"We're being chased," Naomi said in that emotionless operative tone she liked to use when shit went sideways. "Someone must have followed him and his wife to the farmhouse."

"Not them." Josh swore. "Ace."

As if to emphasize that fact, the car went through a serious of maneuvers that had them bracing. Naomi's breath came in gasps.

"I need to get out and see what's going on," Josh told her. "Stay inside this casket, you hear me?"

Gunfire hit the vehicle, glass exploded. Naomi screamed, and the sound echoed in his ears, sharp like a cornered animal's.

With his free hand he tried to lift the lid, but found it wouldn't move. He grunted, jamming his hand and a foot against it. "Come on!"

No dice.

"He's locked us in here, the bastard."

Naomi started pressing on it with him, her panic rising. As they continued to be propelled through streets they couldn't see, Flynn's techniques sent their box banging into the casket next to them.

"I'm going to kill him," Josh said, praying he got the chance.

Naomi stopped beating on the lid, shifting so she could see him. She fisted his shirt. "*I'm* going to kill him when we get out of here."

He chuckled at her echoing his own declaration. "Well, get in line, baby girl. I get first dibs."

"You shouldn't have stopped me. You should have let me go to Mordecai."

He wasn't going to argue, that was pointless. She'd brought it up in order to pick a fight. Her way of releasing unspent energy. "I'm not letting you out of my sight again, so get used to it."

She took the bait. "You have no control over me. I could disappear forever."

"I'll track you to the ends of the earth. You're not the only badass around here, you know."

"My pinkie is a better operative than you."

He laughed in her face even though he couldn't quite make out her features. "We survive this, and I'm gonna make you prove it."

Their mouths were so close, he could've kissed her, and in the darkness, he sensed more than saw her glaring at him. "Exactly how do you think you're gonna do that?"

"Whatever test you want to throw at me, bring it on. I'll take that challenge and you'll see."

They continued arguing who was better for another few minutes, and suddenly, Josh realized they were no longer taking curves at high speed or dodging bullets. The hearse had slowed.

He tried the comm unit again. "What the hell happened back there?"

This time Julia responded. "Hang tight. We're almost to the location."

Josh smacked the speaker and sighed. Naomi tucked herself in closer to him, nestling her head under his chin. "Don't think I don't know what you were doing, trying to get my mind off being stuck in a casket with you."

"I can think of better things to do than argue with you in

close quarters like this, but I figured that was the best route to take."

She pinched his chest. "You're a bastard."

He chuckled and kissed the top of her head. "Yeah, but you love me."

It was meant as a flippant comment, but he felt her stiffen.

"Don't get all mercurial on me now," he said. "I know you don't actually love me, nor do you want any kind of relationship, you're a badass assassin, blah blah blah."

She pinched him again and he yelped, which made her laugh, and that made it worth it. "You know what the word mercurial means?"

It was his turn to pinch her. "Are you implying I have a limited vocabulary?"

"Goats usually do."

"You're impossible, you know that?"

"Yes, but you love me anyway," she said in a sultry voice.

He held her close then until they felt the hearse bump and drive down into what Josh assumed was an underground parking area. The vehicle slowed, came to a stop, and they were removed from the back end while still inside the casket.

"Why isn't he letting us out?" Naomi whispered when it became obvious they were being transported on a gurney.

"Hang tight. As soon as it's safe, he will."

When Flynn opened the lid, Josh and Naomi blinked at the bright lights that assaulted them. Josh sat up and helped her climb out, the two of them staring at a bare room constructed of concrete walls. There was nothing but the casket, a table bolted to the floor, and two chairs. Those were also bolted down. "What is this?" Josh asked.

Flynn motioned at Ace to leave. "You need to go with Julia," he said to Josh. "Stone wants to talk to you."

"Can I have my box, man?" Ace asked.

Flynn gave him a *get lost* look.

"Okay, okay." The mortician backed away. "I'll pick it up later."

Julia motioned for Josh to follow her. "We need to go."

He grabbed Naomi's hand. "I'm not going anywhere without her, and especially not until you tell us what's going on."

Naomi squeezed his hand. "First, we want to know who chased us."

Another man entered, dressed in a tailored suit. He slapped a photo on the table. "Truman Gunn," he stated, the faintest of British accents ruffling his voice. "Me, not him. Nice to make your acquaintance." He didn't offer to shake. "I'm here on behalf of Director Stone, and I believe this is our culprit on the bike—Colin Barber."

Naomi sucked in a breath. "That flaming bastard."

Gunn straightened the cuffs of his tweed jacket. That thing had to be suffocating, but he looked like he'd walked out of a GQ spread. "My sentiments exactly. I've been tailing him over the past few weeks and he's up to something my government isn't in on. We believe he's involved in criminal activities, the details of which I can't share, but if he's entangled with the recent explosion, or the operative Rahab, we need evidence and we need it soon."

Julia looked to Flynn, who nodded. "He attempted to plant an explosive on the hearse," she told them. "It's possible he's been watching Ace's place to keep tabs on Josh." She pointed to him, then switched to Naomi. "Since the bombing, he may have backed off, but resumed again after your breakout from the embassy."

Josh stared down Flynn. "I'm not leaving Naomi."

Flynn said to Gunn, "Thank you for sharing that. We'll keep you posted."

"It's okay," Naomi said as Gunn nodded his goodbye. "I'll be fine."

Josh didn't look at her. "You said you were bringing us to a safe house."

Flynn's face was expressionless. "I believe what I told you was that I was going to keep you safe, and this is the place to do it. It may not look like much, but no one's going to find you here."

Julia glanced at his and Naomi's connected hands, their shoulder-to-shoulder stance. "Naomi will be safe; I give you my word."

Naomi broke their hand hold and nudged him. "Go with her. I can hold my own with Director Flynn."

He knew it wasn't just bravado, but that she truly believed she could deal with his boss. A spark of pride warmed his chest. He kissed her forehead. "I'll be back as soon as I can."

It felt wrong to leave her, but on the other hand, he wanted her to know that he believed in her. As he walked down the cold, bleak concrete hall behind Julia, he had the twinge between his shoulders that told him this place was familiar.

He'd been in one of these rooms before, being grilled before his first field assignment. One last parting test to make sure he'd never give away information to the enemy.

He'd passed then.

Would he pass now?

Upon entering a room at the end, as bare as the previous one, he found Michael Stone sitting at the table. The Deputy Director of the CIA scanned him from head to toe, disgust in the hard lines of his face. "What the ever loving fuck have you gotten yourself in to?"

21

U*nknown Location*

"HAVE A SEAT," DIRECTOR FLYNN SAID.

Naomi eyed the metal chair. She wanted to refuse, but it seemed she was past the point of being argumentative just for the sake of it.

Still, she stayed standing, leaning one shoulder against the concrete wall and crossing her arms. "Who sent Barber? You know, don't you?"

He nodded, but didn't offer to answer.

Fine. She went to the table and sat. "What is it you want from me?"

"Exactly what I told you earlier. I will do whatever it takes to keep my operative safe. I'd let you go, but I know Josh will go after you and end up dead. Whatever we decide to do here, he's part of the plan, understand?"

She did. "I'll tell you what I know about Rahab, but it isn't a lot."

Her agreement garnered her an answer. "The Brit was most likely sent by your grandfather."

"He tried to kill us!"

Flynn shrugged. "Possibly. Mordecai may have sent him to kidnap you, or at least scare you."

"I can't..." *believe it.*

The unsaid words hung in the air.

"You can fill Julia in on Rahab when she returns." He pulled papers from inside his jacket and unfolded them before handing them to her. "All I care about is that you hunt the woman down for me."

She accepted the papers and scanned them quickly. "Asylum?"

"Are you really planning to go back to Israel, to Mossad? Your grandfather may not kill you, but I don't think he's going to let you off easy after what you've done to defy him and screw up his plans."

"So you think offering me this will get me to come work for you?"

"I'm giving you what you need to complete a job and keep yourself and Josh alive. If you want to look at it as manipulation, so be it, but I see it as a way out for you. The only way out."

She studied his features, the set of his shoulders, his calm demeanor either real or carefully practiced.

They glared at each other for a long moment, and she knew he had to be as stubborn as she was.

She could outlast the best of them, never breaking eye contact. Lesser men faltered, backed off. Like Josh, she suspected Flynn would never do either.

"If anyone from Mossad wants to come after me, you can't protect me. Or Josh," she added.

"You were right to have us show the world he was dead;

I'll give you that. Even if you choose to refuse this offer, I will keep him safe. You may think Kidon and the Mossad infallible, but I know differently."

Sensing a story behind that claim, she wondered if she could hear it at some point. What would it be like to stay in America, stay with Josh? What did it feel like to be safe, not looking over your shoulder twenty-four hours a day?

Her, work for the CIA though? Never, but what *would* she do? Get some minimum wage position at a pizza place? Become a suburban housewife?

Laughter bubbled under her breath. She'd never been that type of person. She craved the rush, the adrenaline, the knowing that she was important to her family, to her country. That didn't leave a lot of room for part-time work or housewifery.

Director Flynn seemed to understand her conundrum, and he leaned forward with his elbows on the table and looked at her as if they were old friends. "With your skills, we can find you a challenging and exciting job that will still keep you out of the spotlight."

She shook her head and rolled her eyes, getting up to pace on her painful ankle. "If I don't agree to this, will you let me go?"

"I can't, Naomi. Like I said, Josh will go with you and you'll both wind up dead."

"Then what happens to me?"

He must have seen the fear in her eyes that she might land in a cell like this for the rest of her life. "I'll force you to go to work for me. You don't want that, and honestly, neither do I. But, if I have to keep you under my thumb to keep an eye on you and keep Josh safe, then that's what I'll do. You can train initiates at The Farm, or work with Julia in counter-intelligence."

She put a hand over her face and groaned. No way would she let him see that a part of her actually found that appealing. Training operatives to go into the field undercover? She'd never considered it before, but she'd be a hell of a good teacher.

"You're a focus person." Conrad stood and paced as well, brushing back his jacket to put his hands on his hips. "You may be an initiator, like Julia claims, but once you lock on to a mission or a person, you refuse to be distracted. You have tunnel vision. From what I know, combine that with being an initiator, you could do just about anything you set your mind to."

"Are you labeling me?"

He ignored the question. "Right now, you need to set your mind to survival, but also think about your future. I can help you with both. You have to stop seeing the micro world and look at the macro. This is a hell of an opportunity for you."

And for Josh. When she looked at the big picture, like Flynn and his wife kept talking about, all she saw was him.

The director faced her. "I want you locked on bringing Rahab to justice. You'll be working with Josh, because he needs to be locked onto something as well, and as long as this is your mission, it will be his, too, regardless if I tell him to do it or not. He needs this as much as you do, to relieve his guilt over the death of those in that building. Not only would you be bringing an assassin to justice, you'd be helping your boyfriend get his head back on straight."

It sounded good, but she needed to think about it. She was exhausted, the pain in her ankle a constant distraction, as well as Josh's absence. She went to the table and scanned through the papers, seeing the sections for her signature and the date. "If I defect, my grandfather will have me killed."

"I'll handle Mordecai," Flynn told her.

She stared at the two sheets, seeing her future on that blank line, just waiting for her commitment.

She slid the papers back to him. "I need a few minutes to think it over."

Flynn nodded, leaving the offer, and tossing an ink pen on top. "Don't wait too long."

❧ 2 2 ❧

Josh was cold, hungry, and pissed off when Julia finally came to get him hours later.

He'd talked his way out of being fired, Stone sounding like his former Marine drill sergeant as he gave Josh a lecture he would never forget.

Julia left him at Naomi's cell, unlocking the door. "There's a lot riding on her cooperation," she murmured softly. "I know the two of you are under an extreme amount of stress, but this could all be over shortly if we can come to an understanding."

Josh made a non-committal noise and walked in, stopping when he saw Naomi asleep in the corner.

Julia closed the door behind them, and he listened for the lock falling into place. It didn't come. He was both surprised and relieved, and wondered at the chain of events that had led him to this moment.

Stone had told him about the offer of asylum. As Naomi continued to doze, her exhaustion evident in the fact she didn't wake at his presence, Josh saw the set of papers on the table. Sure enough, her signature was on the second sheet, along with the date, and relief flooded him. He debated whether to disturb her, then gave in, because really, what was the point of trying to stay away? He couldn't. He needed to touch her, hold her.

She woke, but didn't say a word, melting in to his body when he crawled in beside her. Within minutes, she fell back to sleep.

He closed his eyes and did the same, waking later to the sound of the door opening.

Flynn and Julia walked in with an assortment of clothes and two backpacks. One was Josh's new gray one. The other was nearly a match to it, and both were bulging.

Naomi jerked awake, natural instincts kicking in. She jumped to her feet, looking like she was ready to wrestle a bear.

"Hey, it's okay," he soothed, rubbing his eyes and standing as well.

She blinked, looked bewildered for a moment and then accepted a Styrofoam cup of coffee from Julia. "Thanks."

Julia had also brought food, and they descended on the items as Flynn laid out a plan for what they were about to do. Josh listened intently, and then made suggestions.

Deputy Director Stone came in with Mac McDonald. McDonald nodded at Josh and handed each of them an envelope. Josh's contained an assortment of gadgets, Naomi's held a new ID and supporting documents.

Michael Stone looked her over. "If you remove the GPS trackers or try to disable anything in order to run, I will descend on you like an air raid, and you will disappear to a black prison that makes this room seem like paradise. Capisce?"

Naomi tapped her new passport on the table, appearing as

if she was ready for that bear again, and Josh braced himself. "I signed the damn papers, and I am cooperating on all fronts. Threats do not work on me, so drop the tough guy routine. I'm doing this of my own free will, and because it involves Josh's life, as well as mine, I will not fail. I certainly have no intention of sabotaging the mission."

Flynn glanced between all of the players. "Can we get on with this now? You can resume the pissing match after Josh makes the call."

Stone gave him a hard stare but motioned at him to do his thing. Flynn pulled out a familiar cell phone—Naomi's—and punched in a number. Seconds ticked by and when the person on the other end answered, he gave Josh the go signal.

Josh assumed a power stance, anchoring his feet and sticking out his chest as though Mordecai were across from him. "I have your operative."

Flynn put the phone on speaker and Josh held his breath.

No one responded.

Naomi gripped the back of the chair, eyes glued to the phone. It had to be Mordecai on the other end, but only dead silence met their ears.

Her eyes glanced up at him. He could see her fear, her desperate need for her grandfather to answer and say he'd do anything to get her back.

The old bastard did no such thing.

Flynn quirked his mouth as if this were a game he enjoyed. He motioned a finger in the air. *Get on with it.*

"I'll break her in less than twenty-four hours," Josh told the Mossad leader, wondering if the man realized who he was speaking to. "I'm sure she'll tell me things you'd rather your ally, the United States, didn't know."

Another quiet moment. Josh's heart hammered. What the fuck was this dude up to? How could he be so cold, so heartless?

Finally, there came a sigh, then a scoff. "You can't break my granddaughter," Mordecai replied. "She was trained by the best."

"I can and I will," Josh countered with total confidence. "And you and I know that you're not the best, although I'll give you credit for being one of them. I'll take great pleasure in breaking her, since she tried to kill me."

A hush fell again. Josh wanted to bang his fist into the table, throw his coffee across the room.

Instead, he reined in his anger, touched Naomi's hand.

He saw her swallow hard but her grip on the chair eased. She leaned her shoulder into him.

Flynn gave Stone an exasperated look, shook his head and toyed with the phone.

Josh had to up his game if this was going to follow the script Flynn had outlined. "After I get every last bit of info I can extract, I'll send her home to you. Piece by piece."

Naomi raised her brows and shot him a glare. She wanted to say something but instead flipped him off. He grinned.

"What is it you want?" Mordecai asked.

Flynn's grin broadened for a second, he winked at Naomi.

She flipped him off, too.

Josh schooled his face again, all business. "There's a bookstore on the north side of town called Tangerine Dreams. Three p.m. today, outside patio. I'll give you her location once you agree to my terms. If not? Well, we'll see how cooperative your granddaughter is when she finds out you tried to kill her."

The other end of the line went dead without a denial to that accusation. Naomi deflated, and he thought he saw the hint of tears. He grasped her hand and interlaced his fingers through hers.

Flynn shoved the phone in a pocket. "You're on."

"Thanks," Josh said. It seemed weird to say it. "Do *not* show up at the meeting."

His boss gave him a shocked expression, totally faked. "Please. I have no desire to die, and Mordecai would be happy to take me out. But this should flush out Rahab. The rest is up to you two."

❈ 23 ❈

W*ashington, D.C.*

"Rahab is using a secret entrance to get in and out of the embassy," Naomi told Josh. "I'm sure of it. I didn't even realize it was there until they dragged me to the basement yesterday. That must be how she's meeting with my grandfather."

He was driving the rental again, and Del was on the vehicle's Bluetooth speaker, the sound of furious typing in the background. "Gotcha! The original blueprints show a rear exit in the basement with a tunnel that leads to a shop a block over. Give me a second..."

She scanned the map on the tablet Director Flynn had supplied, accessing the layout of the area of the city they were heading to.

"Goddess Garments," Del told them. "And that business is owned by a corporation called Levy Manufacturing."

"We need eyes on that," she said, "and check if Levy is connected to any of our players."

"I'm on it," Del told her.

Naomi stared at the screen without seeing it. "She was right under my nose and I didn't know it."

Josh reached over and grabbed her leg, giving it a jiggle. "Don't beat yourself up. The cards were stacked against you. You thought she was dead."

She kept thinking about her grandfather—how could he betray her? It cut like a knife. She hadn't realized she could feel such pain.

Del directed them to a hotel a quarter mile from the bookstore. Josh pulled into a community parking lot, gathering a sports bag from the trunk. Naomi took both of their backpacks. He also carried a guitar case, but there was no musical instrument inside.

She hurried to keep up with him, the overcast sky and cold wind going right through her jacket. On the hotel's rooftop, Josh set up a rifle and scope. Naomi, beside him, used binoculars to watch the outdoor patio.

Over the next twenty minutes, people came and went, a few brave souls stopping to sit outside and read. Neither Flynn, nor any other operative that she could identify, was in sight. The whole scene was...normal.

As if a wanted terrorist wasn't in their midst. As if the explosion hadn't happened.

A red Maserati pulled in to a parking space on the street a block down. A man emerged from the store and walked down the sidewalk to the car.

Completely normal. The back of her neck tingled.

He climbed in and it pulled away. Lazily, purring like a cat.

Nothing unusual at all.

"Damn it," Naomi said. She wanted to kick herself.

Josh adjusted the scope, scanning the area. "What?"

"That was Rahab."

"In the Maserati?"

She shoved the binoculars in her bag. "Mordecai must have told her we'd be here."

Del's voice came through their ear pieces. "Should be easy to track that car via street cams."

"Not the driver." Naomi responded to Josh, helping him with the scope. "The man who came out of the bookshop. She disguised herself. I'm sure of it."

The time for the meeting had come and gone. As suspected, her grandfather hadn't showed and Rahab had.

Josh began packing up the rifle, his movements tight. She couldn't tell if he was annoyed at her, or at himself. She didn't say anything as they returned to the car, stowing the equipment.

It didn't take long for Del to get a hit, and soon they were driving out of the city and into the burbs.

"Traffic cams are hit and miss in this area," Del told them. "You're going to have to scan for it."

Five blocks later, they saw the flash of red. It was parked outside a large Victorian with an assortment of white and yellow flowers lining the sidewalk that led to the front door. They cruised past, Naomi reeling off the house's number.

Parking a good ways down the block, they waited for Del to uncover the owner. "Sol Meadori. He's a professor who teaches Middle Eastern history and is outspoken about the politics of the region."

"Do you recognize that name?" Josh asked her.

"Never heard of him."

Their phones lit up with a photo of the man. "This is from the University website," Del said.

"That's the professor?" Josh stared hard at the groomed man in the picture, very different and years younger than the man he'd seen a few days ago. "He was at DeValdi Industries the other day, arguing with the doctor in the stairwell. I stumbled on them during a break. I thought he was an employee, but maybe they're friends or lovers. It was definitely a heated exchange."

"That's how he figured it out." Naomi felt the pieces snapping into place. "Meadori may have been on Papa's radar already, because of his politics. DeValdi told Meadori about the cyber weapon, he told Rahab, then she went to my grandfather. Or Mordecai found out about it from Barber, and then targeted Meadori to get to DeValdi."

"Not lovers." Del cleared his throat. "The two men are half-brothers. Also, Meadori's financials show he's had several large deposits hit his bank account, definitely more than a professor's salary, but I can't tell where they came from." Typing ensued. "Okay, wait... Looks like it may be a shell company of Levy Manufacturing. He's been funneling some of the money to a political party in Israel. One that demands the country leave the United Nations and break ties with America."

Josh's phone buzzed with a second incoming call. "It's Flynn."

He put the director on speaker and Naomi's stomach sank as she listened. "Mordecai called. He's changing the game plan. I want you two back at the bookstore by four."

Her grandfather was calling the shots now.

❈ 24 ❈

Conrad couldn't help it, he had to be there.

He'd warned Josh and Naomi when they'd discussed his plan that Mordecai would do this—change the details so he could control the environment.

So, to Josh's dismay, he was with them this time. His adrenaline was rising, and he could at least get a small fix by being involved. He could also watch his operative's back in case things went sideways.

Not with Rahab and Mordecai—with Naomi.

He still couldn't bring himself to totally trust her, and he knew Josh was beyond reason when it came to her.

Conrad had plenty of associates who owed him favors, and sneaking Ace in as a store clerk took all of ten minutes. He also had McDonald disguised as a nerd, sitting at a patio table reading a book.

Waiting and watching was always the hardest part, but the three on the roof were no strangers to it. He expected Naomi to be the most anxious, but she showed nothing, whether for his benefit or Josh's he didn't know.

At the designated time, neither Mordecai nor Rahab were

anywhere to be seen. Josh and Naomi searched every face, every person, every item anyone carried, looking for the tell-tale sign of a disguise. They were all on high alert, and then the unexpected happened, as it so often did.

"Wait, that's the professor."

Del had provided all of them with a photo of Meadori. Conrad adjusted his binoculars to zoom in on the unassuming man. He was dressed a lot like McDonald, except he wore a bow tie. He entered the store.

"You're on," Josh said to Ace. "Don't blow it."

Inside, Ace reassured them. "I got it, man. Ease up already. He's perusing the new releases section." A pause. "Now he's headed for...boring land...history."

Conrad prayed his plant wasn't obviously following the guy around, but he at least told them what was happening. "Don't lose sight of him."

"Dude likes big books, that's for sure," Ace murmured. The sounds of the bookstore echoed in the background. "Wait, we're on the move again. Seems he's also got a thing for...muscle cars?"

Josh, Naomi, and Con exchanged a look. Conrad scratched his head, wondering if there was some kind of message being exchanged between Meadori and another person inside.

"Has anyone approached him?" Naomi quizzed Ace.

"No one's even given him a second glance," the mortician confirmed.

As they listened, keeping an eye out for any of their other players, the professor bought a fancy tea, along with a book and a magazine, and returned outside. He sat at one of the tables not far from Mac, sipping his beverage and leafing through the magazine.

"Hold up," came Ace's voice. There was a smattering of noise, the opening and closing of a door and the flip of a lock.

"One of the other clerks gave me a slip of paper with an address on it. Told me a customer said to give it to the guy with a bow tie. What should I do?"

The three of them said in unison, "Take it to the professor!"

"Right."

"What's the address?" Conrad asked.

He rattled it off, and Del chimed in. "Looking it up now."

Ace appeared below them, finding the man and handing him the slip of paper before returning inside.

"See if you can confirm who the customer was from them," Conrad said. "I want to know who gave her the paper."

On the patio, Meadori read the address, then pulled out a cell. He appeared to text someone.

"I've got him!" Ace's voice was excited. "He's going out the back."

Conrad jumped up. "Do not pursue, you hear me? Do. Not. Pursue."

His phone buzzed as he was about to go down the fire escape and see if he could catch the guy.

"I sent you a picture of him," Ace said.

Naomi and Josh looked at their phones, same as Conrad.

"I'll be damned," he said to himself.

"That's him." Naomi held up hers with the picture on it. "That's Barber!"

Rahab, Barber, Meadori. What the hell was going on here?

This was it. He could feel it in his bones. Conrad nodded at Josh and Naomi. "We're a go."

❦ 2 5 ❦

M*aryland*
The address led to an abandoned warehouse once home to a steel company that specialized in boat hulls. They'd passed numerous golf clubs and parks, leading out of the city and into the country. Fences, barns, and horses were plenty.

As Naomi, Josh, and Director Flynn staked out the perimeter of the enormous building to find a covert way in, Naomi heard the professor's voice echoing off the tall open ceilings. "Leona? Are you here? What's with the cryptic message to meet you?"

She carefully crawled through a broken window, the shadows inside the warehouse playing with her vision. This section was far enough from the main entrance to not give away her presence, and hopefully allow her to watch what was about to take place. Flynn had made her swear not to intervene. As soon as he could confirm Rahab was on sight, he'd call in the FBI.

She made sure not to step on the broken glass lying on the

ground as she eased to the floor. Dust motes floated in the hazy light coming through spiderwebs, thick and numerous.

Carefully, she made her way around one of the giant skeleton hulls, time and the elements turning portions of it rusty. Lichen and errant flowering weeds had made their home in cracks and crevices, ivy trailing up a banister.

The inside was as big as a ballfield, with many machines and other equipment blocking her view. They helped hide her as well, but she had to be extremely careful of the random tools and other debris spread helter-skelter on the floor. With her bad ankle and the poor lighting, she could end up on her ass in a heartbeat, and worse, give them all away.

If Rahab didn't show, or got scared off, they'd be back to ground zero.

One of the weapons Flynn had supplied was an item that looked like a flashlight, but could stun a three hundred pound person if necessary. It did offer various levels of LED light and Naomi finally had to break down and use the lowest setting to navigate through a series of dark rooms toward the sound of Sol, who was still calling for someone named Leona.

It had to be Rahab, but why had she wanted him to meet her here?

Josh had noted that the Maserati was parked outside in clear view. Didn't seem like Rahab was taking necessary precautions to keep her identity hidden, yet, in reality, maybe she believed that everyone thought she was dead. They had, after all, thought so, up until two days ago.

"What's going on here?" Sol asked.

He was close and she pulled up short, clicked off the light, and held her breath. Had he seen her?

"You don't want to get too close to this," a man replied.

She knew that voice. Peeking around the corner of a large hull, her blood turned to ice. Sallow light streamed through an upper level window that was still intact, and in the spot-light sat her grandfather on a wooden chair.

The professor stepped in front of him and Mordecai moved nothing but a finger, pointing it toward the floor at his feet. "You should run now. As fast as you can."

Naomi's gaze dropped to where he pointed, and her heart stuttered. There was a simple looking device under the chair, two ugly wires snaking up to the underside of the seat.

A bomb.

Rahab strolled into view, her hair and face resembling nothing of the woman Naomi had once known. It was the walk that gave her away—she'd always had a pronounced strut.

That happened when you thought yourself invincible.

"You can come out now, Naomi," Rahab's voice rang out, echoing off the high ceilings.

Naomi knew Josh would be pulling up short, wherever he was, realizing her cover had been blown.

But had that been her plan all along? Had she played a game to draw Naomi here?

Maybe none of this was about DeValdi or Disruption. Or about which country had the most power, or who might be able to stop Rahab from completing an even larger mission.

Maybe it was all about revenge.

Keeping the flashlight loose at her side, Naomi straight-ened to her full height. Everything in her went deadly calm. She walked out from her hiding place, forcing herself not to hobble.

Always show strength, her grandfather had drilled into her. *Never fear*.

"There you are," Rahab said.

Her grandfather swore in their native tongue. Naomi didn't so much as glance at him.

Sol frowned, his gaze ricocheting off her and back to the device. "Leona, what's going on here? I don't under—"

Bam! It was the last thing he would ever say.

Naomi refused to flinch or in any way react. She might be about to meet the same fate, but she'd do it with her head held high.

Rahab laughed. "I needed to clean up a few loose ends, but you were a good girl to follow him here. I thought it would take you longer to figure out I was in town, but everything's worked out well." She cupped Mordecai's shoulder. "Papa, here, has been such a help."

Naomi met her grandfather's gaze, but couldn't read anything but love in his eyes. That, and disappointment.

In her? In himself?

"Don't worry," she told him. "All is well. A wise person..."

She let him finish the rest of the Talmud's words. It was something he had said to her a dozen times in her youth, many more when she became an adult and chose to join him in the profession.

The corner of his mouth moved. A quick, furtive gesture, but she understood it. *Message received.*

Rahab strolled around Mordecai. He wasn't tied up, but Naomi guessed there must be a pressure plate on his seat. If he moved, even shifted his weight the slightest bit too much, it would trigger the device to explode. She leaned down to put her lips next to his ear. "I loved you, old man, like you were my father. I'll always keep a place of honor in my heart for you."

Another person emerged from the shadows. "Come on, my dear," Colin Barber called. "Let's wrap this up and get the hell out of America. Such a depressing place."

If she could, Naomi would have strangled him. "You betrayed us."

He gave her a dismissive smile. "Had a racking good time doing it, too. You should have been nicer to me."

Bam! Barber's face went slack, blood blooming on his shirt. His wide eyes went to Rahab as he stumbled back, hitting a steel beam. He tried to grab on to it, but failed, falling to his knees. "But I..." His voice became garbled. "I loved..."

He fell to the floor.

Naomi started shaking. She and her grandfather were next. Where were Josh and Flynn?

Didn't matter. She had to push her fear aside. "Whatever you want, I'll help you get it. Just let my grandfather go."

Rahab let the gun hang by her side, looking Naomi up and down. "*You* are what I want. And before you believe the worst of me, I actually did kind of like him." She waved the gun in Barber's direction. "Ironic, huh? The two of us, big bad Kidon assassins, falling for smart-assed spies? At least, I knew not to let mine get in the way."

Naomi needed to get closer in order to use the weapon in her hand, but she knew any move she made could trigger Rahab to react. "I'm sorry about what happened. It wasn't meant for you."

Rahab wasn't appeased. "But you *did* poison me. Hurt like a bitch, too. I thought I was dead—I actually wanted to die at one point."

She paced once more behind Mordecai, her gaze on Naomi like a sly cat, sizing up the mouse she was about to pounce on. "Out of chaos comes order, though. It gave me a brilliant idea. What better way to live a life of freedom than to stay deceased? I knew if Mordecai found out I had deceived him, I'd be dead for real, and I got tired of it hanging over my head. I needed to draw him out, and you, too, in order to finally succeed."

"You'll never succeed," Mordecai told her.

Naomi saw Rahab's face morph right before she raised the gun.

She screamed at the top of her lungs, a distraction that worked only for seconds, but it was enough. With Rehab's startled gaze on her, Naomi launched herself at the woman.

The flashlight hit Rahab's hand holding the gun. The weapon went off, sending a bullet into the high roof. Josh charged from the shadows, yelling Naomi's name, as the two of them hit the littered ground hard.

Rahab struck Naomi with her free hand. "You bitch," she cried, but the last word went fuzzy when Naomi jammed the stun gun into the woman's side and fired.

Rahab spasmed and Naomi rolled off. Josh was there, jerking the gun from Rahab's hand before Naomi could blink.

It was all over in seconds, and yet it wasn't.

Mordecai still sat on the bomb.

As Rahab went limp, Director Flynn was at Mordecai's side, telling him he'd already called for a bomb squad.

Naomi wanted to fall on her grandfather and wrap her arms around him, but she was afraid to even touch him for fear she'd end up killing them all.

"I am well, granddaughter," he reassured her. "You still owe me dinner."

She laughed in spite of herself, her nerves raw and needing release. "Don't you think for one minute you're getting out of it, either. You have a lot of explaining to do."

Federal officers arrived, sirens blaring, and Josh handed Rahab over to them. As they led her out of the warehouse, a SWAT team pulled up.

Doors slammed and Naomi drew Josh over to the chair. "Papa, I want you to meet my friend, Josh."

"About time we had a face to face," Mordecai said to him.

"I'd offer to shake your hand, but under the circumstances..." Josh smiled.

Mordecai did not return it. "Once I am off of this contraption, we will have a discussion about how you're going to treat my granddaughter."

Before Naomi could respond that she could take care of herself, an explosion rocked the building from outside.

Josh, Naomi, and Flynn ran to the entrance. Men and women yelled. Smoke climbed into the air, the Maserati lying in pieces.

As agents and officers scrambled to help those injured, one of them yelled, "Prisoner fleeing!"

Through the smoke, Naomi saw Rahab heading around the side and into a field filled with abandoned boats. She'd rigged the car to blow. As a distraction or to kill Barber if the meet up didn't work out?

Naomi hobble-ran after her. Josh called her name. She glanced back and motioned at the building. "Cut her off!"

He jetted into the warehouse once more. Naomi blew around the corner, running as hard as she could. Was her grandfather on some kind of ticking bomb, too?

While they weren't her specialty, she knew enough. Rahab could trigger it with a cell phone. A pager. A handheld detonator.

She had to push the thought away, and be the focused agent that Flynn had labeled her. All she saw was Rahab fleeing into an area Mother Nature had tried to take back on the south side of the building. Trees, weeds, and trailing vines covered what was once concrete, the roots of trees busting up the foundation in places, making it challenging to run over.

The buckled ground aided her. Rahab twisted an ankle, fell, jumped back up. But she swore as she attempted her previous speed. Naomi picked up a chunk of concrete and threw it with all her might.

The rough-edged missile hit Rahab in the calf. Her leg gave out.

Disregarding her own still-painful injury, Naomi thought of her grandfather. Gritting her teeth, she ran all out as Rahab gained her feet once more.

She tackled her and they rolled. Rahab was strong; Naomi equally so. They'd both been trained by Mossad. They knew each other's strengths and weaknesses. While Rahab had been patted down before the officers had marched out of the warehouse, they must have missed the knife she pulled.

The sharp blade cut through Naomi's clothes and into her side. The adrenaline coursing through her body kept her from crying out, the jab barely registering in her mind. All of her training kicked in and she became the honed weapon her grandfather had taught her to be.

The door at the loading dock flew open, smacking into the wall. Josh cleared the ramp, and hauled ass toward them, but he was barely a blip in her peripheral vision. She punched the woman in the nose, kneed her in the stomach, grabbed the fist that Rahab threw and nearly broke her wrist as she twisted her hand in the wrong direction.

The woman bucked and tried to regain the advantage, but Naomi locked her knees around her and flipped her over, face smacking into the rough earth.

And then Josh was pulling her off, the federal officers were there, and Rahab was once more in custody. Her legs felt weak as she watched them lead the snarling assassin away.

Flynn caught up with them. "Your grandfather is safe. The device has been deactivated."

The world tipped for an instant and Naomi grabbed Josh's arm.

The knife was still embedded in her, she realized, when he looked at her with fear in his eyes. "Don't pull it out."

"I'm fine," Naomi said, and then she wasn't, a cold terror once more cramping her stomach.

As a wave of sickness rolled over her, she fell into his arms. She could barely keep her eyes open, an eerie darkness giving her tunnel vision. "Poison," she whispered.

"I need an ambulance," Josh yelled, and he scooped her up and ran.

❧ 26 ❧

W ashington, D.C.

N AOMI FLOATED IN AND OUT OF AN ABYSS, DRIFTING IN A foggy haze. She was warm and boneless, all her cares gone. Memories darted in and out, but the fog chased them off before any could hold her attention.

A soft beeping kept interrupting her dreamless sleep. Faces swam in front of her, then disappeared. Voices sounded far off, fading in and out. When she finally cracked open her lids, she found Josh watching her from a bedside chair. "Hey, baby girl."

His face was blurry and she blinked the fog away. Bits and pieces came back to her. "Hey."

When he saw her eyes, he reached out a hand and touched hers, that familiar way of his fingers trailing over hers, a welcome respite.

"Glad to see you're rejoining the living," he said in a soft voice.

The memories poured in now, making her head ache. She'd maintained consciousness as he'd ridden in the ambulance with her to the ER, demanding she stay with him. Once there, a team of doctors and nurses had whisked her away, taking her into surgery.

The rest was hazy, but she didn't need to remember. She smiled, the rest of her body limp and less able to control. "You can't get rid of me that easily."

He rose and leaned over the bed, kissing her lightly on the lips. "I love you. You may get sick of me telling you that, but you're gonna hear it every day from here on out. You nearly scared me to death, and I'm not kidding. I had heart palpitations."

Her hand was heavy as she reached up to touch his face. "Are you okay?"

"Flynn said it was a panic attack, and he's grounding me for another six weeks at least. Putting me through a bunch of tests to make sure I'm fit for the field. Bastard." There was no menace in it, though. Even in her drugged out state, she could tell he was actually happy to stay put. His next statement told her why. "Guess I'll have to stick around for your recovery, since the doc claims you'll need that same amount of time to heal from the wound in your side."

Thick bandages wrapped around her middle. "Papa?"

"He's fine. The bomb squad was able to defuse the device. He's in the waiting room. Been pacing like a caged tiger."

As if Mordecai knew she was awake, the door cracked open and he stepped inside. Josh squeezed her hand. "I'll leave you two alone for a minute."

She didn't want him to go. She hadn't even confessed she loved him, too, but she did need to talk to her grandfather alone.

Licking her parched lips, she attempted to sit up. He

rushed to the bed and helped her use the button to raise herself. "Don't tax yourself," he said.

She was about to start in on him when he raised his hand to stop the lecture he must have sensed was coming. "I knew you would out think Rahab and stop her. Before you threaten me, you should know I had no idea she was alive until last week. Even then, I never dreamed that she was against us."

"Who was she working for?"

"Both the Americans and Mossad are looking into it, but at this point, it appears she was out only for herself. We have much to investigate when it comes to her and the Brit, but as I understand it, you won't be returning with me to our home."

The asylum. She didn't need it anymore, did she? Her brain was so fuzzy, it was hard to follow all of the threads that seemed to dangle in front of her. "Of course I'll return, if you need me. My agreement with Director Flynn is completed, and he holds no power over me now."

Her grandfather patted her shoulder. "But your boyfriend has some sway, I imagine, and while I've attempted to recruit him for Mossad, he refuses to accept my offer."

Her lips tugged into a grin. "He's very bullheaded. You can see what I've been dealing with."

Another shoulder pat. "An equal match for you, then."

He gave her a few more items of information concerning how Rahab had made it into the country, how she had targeted both the professor and the British spy in her quest to hurt the Americans. She wanted to make it look like Mossad was behind it, and she'd had a lot going in her favor. When she'd seen the opportunity to also exact revenge on Mordecai and Naomi, she had reworked her original plan, drawing them in to the web of deceit and lies in order to wipe her slate clean and start over.

"You should stick to your deal with the CIA," Mordecai told her. "This is your chance to get out of Mossad, to have a life. While I hate to lose you, I want you to be happy, and I think that young man outside is the only person who can truly give you that."

"You said happiness was elusive."

"For me, yes. For you?" He shrugged. "Maybe not."

Her arm felt like a twenty pound weight, but she managed to reach out and grasp his hand. "You'll never lose me."

He bent down and kissed her forehead. "I don't believe you would have left on your own, and I give you my blessing to take this freedom and run with it." He squeezed her hand. "Even if I had told you to leave, you wouldn't have. Part of this is my fault, and I apologize for always putting you in so much danger, but perhaps we can start again. I'm getting too old for this shit."

She laughed. "This 'shit' is in your blood, Papa. You'll never quit."

"I might make a good babysitter, if you ever have children. We'll have to convert Josh, though."

They both laughed at this, but in her mind's eye, she could actually see him taking care of her kids someday. Did she even want any?

While she'd never considered it before, she suddenly did.

Her, a mother. A wife.

But she was still saying no to being a housewife.

He brought her hand to his chest. "Can you forgive me?"

Of course she would, but she wanted him to squirm a little. "I'll think about it."

She'd said it with a smile, so he knew she was goading him.

"You've been cleared of all charges—I told the ambassador and those who needed to know that you were at all times working under my direction. I'll write up the formal dismissal from Mossad as soon as I'm back. By the way, the ambassador was so impressed with your skills in flushing out Rahab in cooperation with the Americans, he'd like to speak to you about a position at the embassy."

She didn't need to ask what that entailed. Sitting at a desk every day and pretending to like meetings? Hard pass. "I'm grateful, but I'm not sure what's next for me."

Except for Josh.

"There will never be another agent like you." Another kiss to her forehead and he left, promising to have dinner with her before he returned to Israel.

A silent tear snuck out from the corner of her eye, and she dashed it away as Josh re-entered the room.

He handed her a tissue. She looked away, dabbed at her eyes, and then wadded the thing up and threw it at him. "Looks like I might be hanging around for a while. Think you can handle it?"

He gracefully climbed into the bed, shifting her with great care so that he could wrap his arms around her. They lay face to face, legs tangled in the blankets. "You're stuck with me," he said. "Whatever happens, you're hanging around for longer than a while. I'm not letting you go, so be prepared."

She had never said the words to many people in her life, but they felt right now. "I love you," she told him, resting her head on his broad chest. She could hear his heart beating under her ear.

"I love you more."

And there it was—the ongoing competition.

She raised her head to look him straight in the eyes. "You better treat me right, or you might find I've poisoned your morning coffee."

He chuckled, moving a lock of hair away from her cheek. "Every day will be an adventure," he said with a grin.

Ignoring her stiff, tired body, Naomi closed the distance

and kissed him hard. Every day *would* be, and she was looking forward to it.

EPILOGUE

Arlington, Virginia, two weeks later

THE JULY 4TH PICNIC AT STONE'S MANSION WAS IN FULL swing. The sun shone bright overhead and sweat trickled down Josh's neck.

He was moving up in the world, he guessed, scoring an invite to the deputy director's shindig. After the past few months, he felt like he'd earned it, but it still made him pinch himself. It could have gone either way—going AWOL and running away with Naomi or pulling off the biggest operation of his career.

It had only been two weeks since the explosion and aftermath, but she was moving like her old self, only once in a while did he catch her rubbing her side or straining while exercising. Her physical therapist was wowed by her progress and Josh anticipated he'd have to hog-tie her soon and haul her to the sessions, because she thought she was fine.

The two of them had temporarily moved into the farmhouse, giving Ace his apartment back when Cari showed up with her aunt in tow. Seemed she *had* freaked about the proposal but only because she wanted her aunt—the only family she had left—to meet Ace and give her blessing. Josh didn't know the details, but seeing Cari hanging on Ace's arm at the backyard barbeque with the engagement ring on her finger was confirmation enough that a wedding was in the future.

"Beer?" Flynn handed Josh a cold one.

"Thanks. How's Operation Mosquito?"

The director glanced at McD, playing frisbee with Lawson Vaughn and Truman Gunn. The Brit was dressed down today in a polo and knee-length linen shorts. Stone's Rottweiler jumped and barked, playing along. "I haven't pulled the trigger yet. Been a little busy."

Josh took a swig. "Think he's ready?"

"Since you asked, I'd like you to take him under your wing and walk him through a few things."

He groaned and squinted at the sloping lawn, but acquiesced. He still owed Flynn. A lot. "Whatever you need, boss."

"Thanks." Flynn cocked his chin at Naomi. "Has she given any more thought to my proposal?"

Josh's eyes lighted on her. She sat in a group with Julia, their hostess, Brigit, and Anya Radzoya, the princess he'd helped rescue from Russia. Anya was now engaged to Smitty, who joined McD and Vaughn playing frisbee. "She likes you, but not enough to work for you."

It was a shame, too, since Flynn had offered to keep Josh stateside teaching recruits at The Farm. Naomi would be a great instructor, and he could see her at work every day. Unfortunately, she didn't like people, and had a hang up about working for the CIA. Brigit was attempting to recruit her for Homeland.

Good luck with that.

He'd never live it down if she did go to work for them. She'd lord it over him that she was at the pinnacle of America's security chain and her work was even more classified than his.

"She'll come around," Flynn assured him with a wink. "I've fast-tracked her dual citizenship papers, but if you marry her, it'll be even faster."

A plume of smoke engulfed Stone at the grill and he fanned it with his metal spatula. The women oohed and ahhed over Anya's diamond as she flashed it in the sun. Cari and Ace chatted with McD and Zara Morgan. Her and Lawson's baby slept in a carrier near Zara's feet.

Marriage. He'd never thought he'd take the plunge, but Naomi had changed all of that. "It has to be her idea. If I bring it up, she'll refuse."

"Why do you think we're having this picnic?"

Josh slanted a glance at him. "You planned this?"

Flynn sipped his beer, scanning the crowd. "You've got several newly married couples, two more ready to commit, and a new baby in the crowd. Family, kin, tribe...doesn't matter what you call it, you're both part of us, and I've never seen two spies more suited for each other than you guys. Naomi's given up a lot to be with you. She needs new friends, a new family."

"What's your angle?"

"Me?" He looked astonished, but Josh could see the light in his eyes. "With Smitty in London, I need someone who can fill in for me once in a while. Stone is working my ass off. I never have a break or get a vacation, and I have a rather important commitment I need to take time for soon." His gaze landed on Julia. "I promised my wife a trip to Rome and a stop off in Paris, which I intend to make good on."

Josh nearly choked. "You want me to fill in as director of operations? Are you nuts?"

"Yes, but also desperate. It would be a trial run for the two weeks I'm in Europe. You're qualified to handle the spies, Del and Katie do most of the office work, and Stone doesn't like you."

Wait, what? "He doesn't?"

Flynn laughed. "Trust me, that's a plus. He actually thinks you're okay, but it's part of his leader personality type to ride your ass."

"Um, okay." Naomi caught his eye and smiled. It was a wicked look that promised Mr. Happy would be very happy later tonight. "Can I think about it?"

"Sure." Flynn raised his bottle. "I need an answer by midnight."

No pressure. Josh shook his head as Flynn headed to the grill to give Stone grief about burning the hotdogs. Naomi broke away from the women and crossed the lawn to his side. "What did he want?"

"Nothing." The day was beautiful and he had the love of his life with him. His ego bloomed a bit at Flynn's offer. It would be fun to tell Naomi he'd gotten a promotion, even if it was on an infrequent basis. For now, though, he just wanted to enjoy her and this new life they were building together.

Stone looked like he was about to threaten Flynn with the flipper, but began loading burgers and hotdogs onto a platter, instead. "Lunchtime!"

Josh took Naomi's hand. "I'm hungry. Let's eat."

Later that night, after the fireworks were done and they'd returned to the farmhouse, she nibbled at his ear in bed. "That was fun. Sort of. I'm not used to being around so many people."

He toyed with one of her nipples, licking at it to make it peak. "What was your favorite mission of all time?"

"Hmm." She ran fingers through his hair. "The one in Russia, rescuing Anya."

"That wasn't yours, that was mine."

She pushed his probing mouth away. "And a good thing I helped or she wouldn't have been there today with that big, fat diamond on her hand."

He relented. "You are correct."

Her eyes narrowed but she allowed him to return to playing with her breasts. "What about you?"

Thinking about past missions wasn't important at the moment, but it was an easy choice. "This one."

"Capturing Rahab?" She sounded bewildered.

"Yep, because it was really all about you—my favorite addiction."

She kissed him, putting lots of tongue in it. "So I've been thinking."

Her tone was serious and he tore his focus away from her breasts. He rubbed a hand over her bare shoulder, propping himself up on his elbow. "About what?"

"Us."

She looked bashful, and his heart triple-timed it. "What about us?"

"Have you ever been to Vegas?"

That left turn caused him to frown. "No, I'm not a gambler. You?"

"I hear they do quickie weddings."

Now his heart stopped. "They are known for them."

Her gaze went to the ceiling, her fingers knotting and fidgeting with themselves. "We'll have to have a formal ceremony later on. My family will insist on it, and since Momma won't travel, we'll have to go to Israel, but I was thinking..."

"Wait." He took her chin and forced her to look at him. "Are you asking me to marry you?"

Her eyes narrowed. "I'm not asking."

Of course she wasn't. She was demanding.

"I mean," she tugged on a piece of his hair, "I've been

waiting patiently for you to pop the question, and I'm tired of it. You said you love me, now prove it."

Oh, he was going to all right. He grabbed her and tugged her body under his, delighting in her squeal of happiness. He kissed her long and deep, then stared into her eyes. "You're all I've ever wanted, baby girl."

"Good, I booked a red-eye. It leaves in three hours."

He laughed. "Can you wait that long?"

She threw her arms around his neck. "I'm sure you'll keep me distracted until it's time to go."

He shifted and found her wet and ready. "Damn straight," he murmured, nudging himself slowly inside her.

Clinging to him, she moaned, moving under his hips and trying to get him to pick up the pace. He gripped her hips and slowed her down, relishing every stroke.

She tried to control her climax, but he'd learned something in the past few days. It wasn't about who came first—it was about spreading the pleasure between them.

He let her do what she wanted, enjoying every touch, every kiss, every whispered plea. They moved as one, stroking, gliding, finding their unbreakable connection in this moment.

And in the end when they rode the pleasure to its peak, they went over the edge together.

Stay tuned for the next Super Agent adventure with *Operation: Undercover Heist*, coming 2022, and featuring Truman Gunn and an international jewelry thief!

READY FOR MORE?

Don't want to miss a single release? Click here and get a FREE story (or two... :))

SEALs of Shadow Force Series

Fatal Truth

Fatal Honor

Fatal Courage

Fatal Love

Fatal Vision

Fatal Thrill

Risk

SEALS of Shadow Force Series: Spy Division

Man Hunt

Man Killer

Man Down

The SCVC Taskforce Series

Deadly Pursuit

Deadly Deception

Deadly Force

Deadly Intent

Deadly Affair, A SCVC Taskforce novella

Deadly Attraction

Deadly Secrets

Deadly Holiday, A SCVC Taskforce novella

Deadly Target

Deadly Rescue

Deadly Bounty

Deadly Betrayal

The Super Agent Series

Operation Sheba

Operation Paris

Operation Proof of Life

Operation Lost Princess

Operation Ambush

Operation Christmas Contraband

Operation Sleeping With the Enemy

The Justice Team Series (with Adrienne Giordano)

Stealing Justice

Cheating Justice

Holiday Justice

Exposing Justice

Undercover Justice

Protecting Justice

Missing Justice

Defending Justice

❧

SCHOCK SISTERS MYSTERY SERIES w/Adrienne Giordano

1st Shock

2nd Strike

3rd Tango

❧

The Secret Ingredient Culinary Mystery Series

The Secret Ingredient, A Culinary Romantic Mystery with Bonus Recipes

The Secret Life of Cranberry Sauce, A Secret Ingredient Holiday Novella

PNR & UF BY MISTY/NYX HALLIWELL

Paranormal Contemporary Romance

Witches Anonymous Step 1

Jingle Hells, WA Step 2

Wicked Souls, WA Step 3

Dark Moon Lilith, Witches Anonymous Step 4

Dancing With the Devil, Witches Anonymous Step 5

Devil's Due, Witches Anonymous Step 6

Dirty Deeds, Witches Anonymous Step 7

Wicked Wedding, Witches Anonymous Step 8

Urban Fantasy

Revenge Is Sweet, Kali Sweet Urban Fantasy Series, Book 1

Sweet Chaos, Kali Sweet Urban Fantasy Series, Book 2

Sweet Soldier, Kali Sweet Urban Fantasy Series, Book 3

Sweet Curse, Kali Sweet Urban Fantasy Series, Book 4

Paranormal Romantic Suspense

Soul Survivor, Moon Water Series, Book 1

Soul Protector, Moon Water Series, Book 2

Cozy Mysteries (writing as Nyx Halliwell)

Sister Witches Of Raven Falls Mystery Series

Of Potions and Portents

Of Curses and Charms

Of Stars and Spells

Of Spirits and Superstition

Confessions of a Closet Medium Cozy Mystery Series

Pumpkins & Poltergeists

Magic & Mistletoe

Hearts & Haunts

Once Upon a Witch Cozy Mystery Series

If the Cursed Shoe Fits (Cinder)

Beastly Book of Spells (Belle)

Poisoned Apple Potion (Snow) - only available in the Black Cat Crossing box set (but it's FREE when you sign up for the Whiskered Mysteries newsletter!)

Red Hot Wolfie (Ruby)

Hexed Hair Day (Rapunzel) 2021

MEET MISTY

USA TODAY Bestselling Author Misty Evans has published over seventy novels and writes romantic suspense, urban fantasy, and paranormal romance. Under her pen name, Nyx Halliwell, she also writes cozy mysteries.

When not reading or writing, she embraces her inner gypsy and loves music, movies, and hanging out with her husband, twin sons, and three spoiled puppies. She's a crafter at heart and has far too many projects to finish.

Don't want to miss a single adventure? Visit www. mistyevansbooks.com to find out ALL the news!

Check out her humorous pen name Nyx Halliwell for magical mysteries https://www.nyxhalliwell.com .

LETTER FROM MISTY

Hello Beautiful Reader!

Thank you for reading this story! It is an honor and a privilege to write stories for you.

I hope you enjoyed this book, and I'd like to ask a favor – would you mind leaving a review at your favorite retailer? I'd really appreciate it, and reviews help other readers find books they will love too.

If you'd like to learn about my other books, sales, and special promotions, please sign up for my newsletter at www.readmistyevans.com.

Grab special edition box sets and get new releases before they come out at retailers by visiting my direct buy website www.mistyevansbooks.com. I have sales and offer NEW RELEASES early and at a discount!! Check it out.

I also have a holistic business, Soul Healing With Misty, and invite you to check out my website www.crystalswithmisty.com for information on my services.

Last but not least, if you enjoy clean, cozy mysteries, visit my pen name www.nyxhalliwell.com to see those books!
Thank you and happy reading!
Misty

www.ingramcontent.com/pod-product-compliance
Lightning Source LLC
Chambersburg PA
CBHW030753200726
48288CB00004B/1160